Books by JOHN HERSEY

A SINGLE PEBBLE)(1956

THE MARMOT DRIVE)(1953

THE WALL)(1950

HIROSHIMA)(1946

A BELL FOR ADANO)(1944

INTO THE VALLEY)(1943

These are BORZOI BOOKS,

published in New York by ALFRED A. KNOPF

A Single Pebble

A Single Pebble

JOHN HERSEY

Richard 1914-

1 9 5 6

n/DD

56-7209

Alfred A. Knopf : *New York*

W

L. C. CATALOG CARD NUMBER: 56–7209

© JOHN HERSEY, 1956

This is a Borzoi Book published by Alfred A. Knopf, Inc.

Published June 4, 1956
Second printing before publication
Third printing, June 1956
Fourth printing, June 1956
Fifth printing, September 1956
Sixth printing, October 1956

PART ONE

The Junk

I became an engineer. I found my way into hydraulics, and not many years along, while still a youthful dam surveyor, I was chosen by the big contracting firm for which I worked to go to China and study the river called by the Chinese "the Great," the Yangtze, to see whether it would make sense for my company to try to sell the Chinese government a vast power project in the river's famous gorges.

This was half my life ago, in the century's and my early twenties; the century and I were both young and sure of ourselves then.

I spent a year preparing myself for the trip. I applied myself to spoken Mandarin Chinese and got a fair fluency in it. I read all I could find on the Yangtze; I learned of its mad rise and fall, of the floods it loosed each year, killing unnumbered people and ruining widespread crops; of its fierce rapids and beautiful gorges, and of its endless, patient traffic of hundreds of junks towed upstream and rowed down by human motive power.

Even after my studies, though, I could scarcely visualize this storied, treacherous river, and being an ambitious young engineer I could only think of it as an enormous sinew, a long strip of raw, naked, cruel power waiting to be tamed. I had much yet to learn.

I took passage on a steamer to Shanghai, and after an impatient month in that transplanted Western city I was able to talk my way onto a British gunboat, the *Firefly*, which was going upriver as far as Ichang, at the gate of the gorges, on a patrol such as British ships were then allowed by treaty to make on certain Chinese rivers on behalf of British business interests in the interior.

The thousand miles from Shanghai to Ichang were long. The landscape was flat; the river was enormously wide and sluggish. Where was the Yangtze's brutal power? I was let down. We made no stops, and everything on board was British and regular, and I witnessed a riverbank China but did not feel it.

We arrived at length in Ichang. I went immediately,

as I had been told to do, to our consul in that city, and because bandits and revolutionaries were said to be harassing the few flat-bottomed steamboats then trading in the gorges above Ichang, he urged me to go upriver not by steamer but by junk, as he thought I would travel unnoticed that way and would have more leisure for my study. And so with his help I arranged a passage with a thin, gaunt junk owner whose Chinese I could understand quite well, for he was a Szechuan man, from Wanhsien, and the Szechuanese dialect is not too far from pure Mandarin.

I was eager indeed to go aboard his boat.

IT WAS the junk's cook who first colored my whole new view of China.

When I made my deal with the owner, he warned me that he wished to start away early the next morning, and I boarded his vessel, with my bedroll and a single Gladstone bag, just after dawn of the following day.

The boat was a *ma-yang-tzŭ*, one of the great upriver junks, a hundred and two feet in length over all, nineteen feet in beam, made entirely of the tough cypress of the Wanhsien district, with a turret-built hull divided by strong bulkheads into fourteen cargo compartments, and carrying on deck abaft the mast its living quarters, a big shelter for the crew and a cabin for the owner on the stern: a craft well designed forty centuries ago.

All appeared to be ready. The cargo of cotton bales was in the watertight compartments below the loose-planked decks; the crew was fully hired on; lines were clear and all that was needed was handy.

But at the very moment when the owner gave the order to cast off from our spar moorings in the foul muck at the riverbank, the cook cried out that he had yet to take delivery of a supply of *pai-ts'ai,* fresh white Chinese cabbage, at the market place. Amid shouts and laughter he jumped from the junk and rushed along the staked-up plank bridge to dry ground, holding in his hand a bag of the owner's coppers. He was a stocky man, with a clean-shaven head, a round face, black eyes very close together, and skin like buffed candlewax. He glanced back at us, grinning, when he reached the shore, and waved the bag of coppers and made the coins tinkle. He looked a rogue.

I thought the errand would take fifteen minutes. But all the crew, I saw, sat down or lay down, and the men occupied themselves, as if for all the day, with gossip, lice-picking, gambling, and snoozing.

A quarter of an hour passed, and a half, and a whole.

I was alert; I kept watching the riverbank and the rows
of mat huts that crowded to the verge of the muck at
the bank. I grew weary, tensely waiting for the cook.

The owner, I saw, was easy. He was playing a game of
little bamboo "stones" with a Chinese girl whom I took
to be his daughter; later I learned that she was his wife.

As nine o'clock was left behind, the preposterousness
of the delay overwhelmed me, and I went in a kind of
temper to the owner and said that I thought he should
sign on another cook and weigh spars and be off.

The owner had a haggard, fine-wrinkled face, which
had been eroded, one could guess, not so much by
weather as by fiercely running thoughts of profit and
loss. From his chin hung a black, sparse beard of hardly
more than a hundred hairs—a token of dignity and idle-
ness. He turned this face up to me and mildly said, in a
phrase I was to hear often spoken by the Chinese with a
shrug and a look of resignation, "There is no way."

So, frustrated in my Western hurry—I *was* in a hurry,
with hundreds of miles of hydro-electric promises ahead
of me—I lay down on the deck and tried to be patient,
listening to the owner sucking at his teeth and to the
low, sweet murmur of his young wife's dutiful laughter
when he spoke to her words I could not make out.

The time shuffled along. Bursts of conversation and

sudden little arguments came from the clump of trackers forward, but they seemed content and laughed often. The hour came and went for the noonday meal, and because the cook had gone ashore it seemed evident that there would be no such lunch: for who would fix it?

At about two o'clock the owner's young wife came, carrying a handleless cup and a pot with a quilted cover, to where I was still lying disconsolate. She poured me some tea without speaking; she looked at my face openly, but she seemed afraid of me. She went back to her husband then and their game went on.

I seemed to be held in a prison of others' patience; I was wild, but I lay still.

It was nearly five in the evening when the cook came aboard. He did not have the cabbages. He did have, in one hand, holding them upside down by their bound legs, four live chickens, and in his other hand he had a big jug of vegetable oil. He was cheerful and possibly drunk; the owner, who was also cheerful, greeted him quietly; the owner's wife acknowledged his slight bow with a slight bow; the crew welcomed him with jokes and friendly curses; and only I seethed. Needless to say, it was too late to set out on the river that night. We stayed at the mooring, and I slept badly among noc-

turnal cries, coughs, spittings, songs, and sounds of the
loading of coal by hand into the bunkers of the *Firefly*
out in the stream.

WE STARTED up the river at dawn the next day.

I carried over into the journey's first morning, like an
aching muscle strained the day before, the painful knot
of impatience that I had built up while waiting for the
cook. These Chinese aboard the junk did everything so
slowly and carelessly!—and with such infuriating cheerfulness. Though they had begun the noisy work of
weighing moorings just as the first incendiary hints of
sunrise had lit up the mists around the strange pyram-
idal hill across from Ichang, it was nearly ten o'clock
by my watch before we finally cleared the pack of
moored junks on the city's lap and began to move upstream. I was outraged by the deliberation of the owner.
He was setting out on a nearly two-hundred-mile voyage with a cargo worth two hundred taels, perhaps more;
surely upstream speed would mean downriver profit for
him. Yet he seemed not to care whether he made twenty
miles or one in his first day's progress. Once in a while
he would rise up in a fury of shouting at his crew; then
he would subside to his tea and his game of "stones"

with his young wife, and it seemed that his outbursts were a matter of form, almost of ceremony.

I noticed the owner's wife more closely than I had the day before, when she had seemed just a rather shabby, though somehow bright and even coarsely pretty young woman of the river. Now I saw that the brightness came from her eyes; when her husband stood up in his formal rampages, her large black-pupiled eyes took in more than his exaggerated presiding gestures and shouting rushes. She looked in the faces of the crew. She saw the men. Her eyes were wide open, figuratively as well as actually, it seemed to me, and they looked wiser than the rest of her young face seemed to warrant.

By mid-morning my irritability, like the mists on the river which were gradually burnt off by the April sun, was dissipated by the all-melting view into the heart of which we were being carried on a fine breeze by our big bamboo-ribbed lugsail. All the way from Shanghai, a thousand miles by river, the terrain had been flat and brown. Now, in a soft spring morning laden with the fragrance of dewy grass and numberless violets, we moved in a northerly direction across what seemed an inland lake nearly three quarters of a mile wide, with sun-washed mountains along the west bank and low purple hills to the east.

Then all at once, on the left, a cleft in the massif showed itself, and there, narrowed to two hundred yards, flowing between rounded limestone mountains, was the Great River in the first of its wondrous gorges. The surprise was overwhelming.

It was here at the mouth of Yellow Cat Gorge that I first saw the trackers at work, as we had too little wind to sail against the constricted current; and it was here, therefore, that I first noticed the head tracker. As the lugsail was taken in and the junk was rowed toward the left bank by a squad of trackers, I noticed that one of them, a lumpy, broad-faced fellow with a shaven head, who was dressed in new blue cotton pants and a drab ragged jacket, took the lead in all that was done. From his powerful larynx to his square feet, this man, whom the owner addressed with a nickname, Old Pebble, seemed to be one whole, rhythm-bound muscle. Everything he did had rhythm. As he gave orders on board the junk, he kicked his feet on the slapping unbolted planks of the deck; he punctuated what he said with tongue-clicks; his hands moved in rope-pulling gestures, all in time with his cadenced speech. His head was spherical, and he had the crow's feet of cheerfulness all the way from his narrow eyes back to his ears. I have never been able to tell with certainty how old a Chinese is; I would guess that this one was in his mid-thirties. At any rate, the "Old" of his nickname was surely an affectionate term; he seemed young and strong. I saw that he wore a silver ring, and although his hands had no more grace than monkey-wrenches, he had let his fingernails grow rather long, in the old style, evidently to show that he was of the boatmen's nobility.

That evening, after we had made perhaps ten miles between amazing limestone battlements, turrets, and buttresses, towed every inch of the way by the chanting trackers, with the one called Old Pebble out in front, singing weird rhythmic melodies—that evening, when we were securely moored in a little eddying cove at the head of Yellow Cat Gorge, I spoke to the head tracker. He received me openly and without deference.

I began to question him about his life.

"I pull the towline," he said, and stopped, as if to say: What more is there? What more could there be?

But, I asked, what of the future?

"I have very little," he said, and he spoke as if having little were the greatest fortune, and the greatest buffer against the future, that a man could wish.

Again I tried to ask him what his goal was.

"In my spare time ashore I drink wine," he said. "I never fight when I get drunk. I just talk when I'm drunk and lean against a wall and go to sleep. I hate fighting, and really no one wants to fight me. I am an 'old good.' I don't save money, I spend it on my friends. I buy them wine. I buy friendship. I save friendship. But some of the men on the river are no good. If they know you have money, they want you to gamble with jumping sticks or cards. If you refuse, they form a circle around you and threaten you."

He cleared his throat and spat over the side into the Great River, and he seemed very pleased with himself.

"What do you want?" I asked.

"I have no home; my body is my home," he said. "But I am an old good. I shall stay on boats, and there will always be someone to hire me, and when I am old, all my brothers in the boatmen's guild and all the captains on the riverside who know me will give me a few coppers in payment for the friendship I have hoarded for them. I will have plenty. I will have a fine funeral."

This was the way he spoke. At the time I wanted to believe him, and mostly did, though I thought him full of guile; in my Occidental complacency I then considered all Chinese liars, anyhow. I guess I wanted to believe that he was a simple, good man, but I was troubled by his obvious inner enjoyment of his account of himself; from time to time he had pursed his lips, so that his face had looked shrewd, as if he had been saying to himself, "I am the grandest liar in the world, and see how I have this stupid foreign boy on my towline!" I thought he might be dramatizing himself as a poor, pure-hearted wanderer, one of Heaven's minstrels, to me, a foreigner who asked questions. I could not imagine that a young, vigorous, and cheerful man could live without distant goals: wealth, family, and a good name widely known.

THE FOLLOWING day, the second of our passage, we moved through a landscape of such wildness as I had never before even imagined. Not far above the cove where we had moored for the night, the river took an abrupt turn to the right, beyond which we entered the trough called Lampshine Gorge. On the bank on our right were steep, giddying limestone cliffs crowned with soft-formed, many-wintered rocks, while on the left, on the shelves of less precipitous but still formidable mountains, picturesque villages and temples rested. Once, high on an apparently inaccessible cliff, we saw huge characters painted on the rock, and the owner read them to me: "The hills are bright, the waters dark." Near the upper mouth of the gorge, on the eastern side, a narrow, isolated pinnacle of limestone

called, as I was told, the Pillar of Heaven rose nearly
two thousand feet; one could imagine that it did, indeed, support the crystal ceiling of the day.

At length we erupted from the gorge. The limestone
formations fell away, and we moved all at once into a
region of plutonic rocks. In a valley nearly a mile wide
huge boulders of gneiss and granite, larger by far than
our junk, lay strewn about, and straight across the line
of the river, relenting only enough to grant it a shallow
channel, curious dykes of greenstone and porphyry rose
up out of the other stone. It was a primeval landscape,
and it seemed to have been arranged by some force of
fury. I was deeply moved and humbled by the sight of
the trackers scrambling like tiny, purposeful crickets
over the rough and intractable banks. We were all hope-
less insects in this setting. My career, engineering,
seemed only nonsense here. Nothing—absolutely nothing—could be done by man's puny will for this harsh
valley littered with gigantic rocks.

By evening I was worn out with awe and small-
stirring fears, for the currents of the river, wrenched
and twisted by hidden boulders and sunken dams of
porphyry, had sucked at our huge junk and made it
tremble and bob as if it had been a mere autumn leaf
on the water; and when, after the evening meal in the
softness of twilight, some slapstick began to be set up

by the cook and the head tracker, while the other men laughed around them, I was irritated. I felt that my boatmates were men without feeling, if men at all. How could they have traveled all day through this land of pre-history only looking forward to an evening of pranks and cackling? The cook and the head tracker jumped about burlesquing the formal ritual of jugglers and magicians, chanting the nonsense-rhymes such men use, and waving their arms and looking mysterious; these two excelled in the universal funny talk of gangs of men—companionable abuse, loving cruelty—and they were making verbal monsters of each other, and their friends roared.

I was sitting cross-legged on some matting, aft, near the owner and his wife. I was close enough to them to hear, now and then, her laughter, which was so low and soft that it seemed to be hardly more than some sort of indulgence—smiling pushed just over the edge into audibility. The owner laughed hard with the rest.

Suddenly the pretended mockery volleying between the two men seemed to become serious. They jumped up, and in the flickering, soft light of paper-chimneyed oil lanterns hanging from the curved overhead ribs of the big fore cabin, their faces glistened reddish and furious; their eyes popped. It was impossible to guess

what had suddenly made the banter of these two vigorous men turn earnest—unless it was the same fury as
had caused the disorder in the great rocks of the wide
valley.

"You are a turtle, the son of two turtles, a bastard
turtle, you!" the cook shouted.

"You are a bastard, I defile your mother!" the head
tracker answered in what seemed to be real bitterness.

What made the quick and ugly change of mood in
the two men eerie was that the mood of the trackers
around them changed not at all. They laughed still, as
if witnessing more of what they had been seeing, and
they laughed no less but no more.

I stood up, for this had turned from an annoyance
into a minor spectacle; it may be that some of my own
feelings, pent all day, were finding a vicarious outlet.

Close beside me I became aware that the owner's
wife was standing, too, in fierce enjoyment of the encounter. Her eyes flashed as she looked at me in the
lantern light.

THE NEXT morning I awoke feverish, and for four days
I lay sick on my bedroll on the planks of the conning
deck, glimpsing only now and then of the passing ter-

rain a rough cliff through the forward arch of the mat roof, seen upside down as I rolled back my head.

High above me on his platform of two planks which partially roofed the deck, the after-helmsman stood, and occasionally I saw his gown or his arm as he sluggishly moved the junk's immensely long tiller. He was a silent, bitter, thin man, whose duties on an upriver voyage were negligible, because the great forward bow sweep, manned by a dozen men, did most of the steering against the current, and I soon thought of the helmsman as a mechanical fixture, a man scarcely there.

I lived to sounds: the beat of the trackers' signaling drum forward of the mast, Old Pebble's faraway chanting and the pained rhythmic cry of the trackers, orders shouted from the junk, the chopping of vegetables, the loud sipping of tea—all the noises of upstream progress; and always along the flanks of our craft the murmuring of the urgent river.

I feared typhoid, but now from this distance I can guess that I was ill of mystification and disappointment, and of a churning up of inner forces I had never known. I had approached the river as a dry scientific problem; I found it instead an avenue along which human beings moved whom I had not the insight, even though I had the vocabulary, to understand. What bothered me, and was incomprehensible to me, was their indolence, their lack of drive, their indifference to goals I held valuable —even to the physical goal toward which we moved without haste, the mid-river port of Wanhsien. So far as I could see, these people had no desire to get ahead. Living day after compartmented day on this primordial river seemed to have done this to them. The central idea of my energetic country meant nothing to them, I thought. Since I had pinned my hopes for China, for an engineered China, upon that idea, I was prostrated, I suppose, as I floated through the awesome terrains of the wild Great River, by what I imagined to have been a terrible discovery—as well as by some trivial germ of that district.

The owner's wife tended me. Her name was Su-ling. She was a nurse of such delicacy—only hinting gentleness, outwardly brusque and rather impersonal—that I felt the impact of her compassion only in the days of my convalescence; but that came later. In the first days of my fever, she would bring me tea and sometimes broth that the cook, she casually told me, had made especially for me. Now and then she gave me news and anecdotes of our trip, none of which really interested me, since a grippal ache in my head and arms and legs took most of my angry attention. She told me once, I remember, that it had required the better part of two days to negotiate Pierced Mountain Gorge and the open valley above it, for there had been a heavy "down-wind" opposing us; her words gave me my only sense of the passage of our craft through days and air and water.

She never touched me, for she was careful, prudish almost, when she was near me. She often put steaming towels on my face to ease the dry discomfort of my feverish skin, letting the hot damp cloths fall across my brow or cheeks and taking care not to brush my face with her fingers. I wondered, when I was somewhat re-covered, what was behind all this. Did it come from what she felt about me? Or from fear of her husband, the owner? Or had she a feeling that I, a white-skinned, long-nosed foreigner in that valley of flat-nosed people, was somehow peculiar and foul?—for I remembered as I lay on the deck of the junk how an otherwise intelli-gent college friend of mine from Alabama had told me once that "niggers have a smell that's different from white people's" and that was fulsome in white nostrils. Was I a fetid, loathsome object to these Chinese? This possibility lay a new deposit on the sense of shock I was storing up, for at home I had been bred to Western superiority, and had thought of China as the home of

the backward Chink, the Heathen Chinee who followed
the wooden plow, the perilous yellow man, a creature
so low that the gates of the sweet land of liberty had
clanked shut in his·face—someone, at best, to be given
a helping hand. Could this simple girl look down
on me?

She was barely twenty, I guess. Certainly her husband was twice her age. She had a slender frame yet
gave an impression of sturdiness, having wrists that
looked good and strong, and a firm neck; I suppose she
had often sculled sampans. Her figure was only to imagine, for she wore blue quilted cotton gowns or, of the
same upholstered material, trousers wrapped with cloth
anklets and jackets buttoned down the side with cloth
knots, and thus she was but a bundle to see; yet I, at
my age, was well able to supply the guesses that
would grace her straight body beneath with goodnesses
enough. Her face was overcast with a shadow, with a
sadness that I frequently saw on the broad faces of the
people who lived on the Great River, a sadness that
came to haunt me—of patience, of acceptance; a sadness that seemed to deepen whenever Su-ling glanced
at the turbulence of the currents through which we
passed. This inner melancholy seemed to be gathered
about one corner of her mouth, on the left side, which

was often drawn tight with a sweet stoic tensity. Her eyes, on the other hand, as I have said, were bright and keen and gay, and when she laughed, as many a time of day she did, they glistened and nearly canceled out the cramp of woe at her mouth. Her hair was coal-black, oily, and not as clean as it might have been—but even that in due course I condoned.

The dreadful idea that she might have contempt for me just because of my foreignness, my otherness, made me try with special zeal, when I had the vigor to do it, to kindle those eyes of hers with amusement and pleasure.

I began to be a little afraid of the men on the boat. I had discovered myself an outsider. Remember, I was only a boy; twenty-four years old. I was young then. I was young. It was good to be young, but who could have told me that?

I became lonely and frightened, yet I remember my convalescence of those days as a poignantly happy period, which I prolonged by will and deceit, feigning misery after it had left me.

The owner came to me in his black coat which was lined with leopard skin and, sucking at his teeth, gave me official permission to submit to his wife's nursing, though I had willingly been doing so for two or three days before he bestowed these oral credentials on me. Thus I was made aware of a watchful eye.

My great surprise of those days was finding the deep, astonishing well of understanding and learning that the river girl had. Su-ling said one afternoon, in her musical murmur, which by then was as pleasant to me as the constant purling of the brown currents against the cypress planks of the junk, that her master had told her that she might recount to me legends and truths of the Ten-Thousand-Mile River, if I wished to hear them, and she seemed to imply that my ignorance of the Yangtze, which I had betrayed with questions, was pitiful and shameful and should be rectified. I urged her to educate me, and was rewarded with extraordinary treasures, poems of Li Po and Tu Fu and myths and dreams and histories. She told me that afternoon, with the sun slanting across her face as she squatted outside the door of the stern cabin, while I lay near her in the open area of the conning deck abaft the great mat arch of the crew's cabinway, a tale of tyranny, of the three generals of the Western Kingdom who swore blood brotherhood in the peachblossom garden of Yang Yuan, and of how after many battles the brother Chang issued an order to the tailors roundabout his camp to make uniforms for his entire army in three days, or perish, and the

tailors were horrified at this impossible task, and some
of them crept, carrying scissors, to the general's room
at night, and his eyes were open and moved about,
frightening them, yet he snored, and hearing his heavy
breathing they pierced his eyes with their scissors and
cut off his head and fled to the Eastern Kingdom; and
that, Su-ling said, with quiet certitude, was why tailor's
scissors were still required to have square ends all over
China. She told her tales, she recited her verse, slowly,
as if deeply impressed with my stupidity, and now and
then, when I could not follow her words, she interpreted
with marvelous pantomime, giving me the word for
scissors, for example, with a lovely crosscutting motion
of her forearms, her leaf-like hands taking the part of
blades, her bright gaze washing me with her desire for
my improvement. I was amazed at the range of her
memory, and its sharp edge, and I began to suffer from
ridiculous feelings of inferiority. I strained to remember
some lines from one of *my* poets; well, there was Whit-
man—*when in the dooryard lilacs . . . when lilacs last
in the dooryard bloomed . . .* How could I render "lilacs," even in pantomime? I protested to myself that
my knowledge was useful; *I* could help to assuage pov-
erty; my knowledge might help one day to make electric
light bulbs cast their healing, teaching glow into every

mat shed clinging to these poverty-washed riverbanks. What was idle verse to that?

Why did this girl, who gave me such delight, fill me also with anger?

Now ONE evening toward the end of my illness I lay on my bedroll watching the crew, and I saw that the head tracker, who had told me that first evening in Yellow Cat Gorge of his scorn for money and belongings and of his hoarding nothing but friendship, was after all able to be greedy just like other men.

We were spar-moored against some big rocks in an eddy between ports. A number of the trackers settled down to a gambling game of jumping sticks, which the head tracker was not obliged, or threatened, or even cajoled to join, but to which he nevertheless did drift, wearing, at first, an indifferent look. On watching his face, however, I began to see in it an alertness to the gaming that later turned into a frantic hungry stare at each man's turn and the exchange of coppers that followed. Finally, squatting on his hams and demanding a turn himself, he took the bamboo receptacle which held the stiff bundle of marked chopsticks from his neighbor, and he jounced the container and rattled the

sticks in his own eccentric, jerky rhythms, behaving as
if he had in his hands some remarkable talisman, some
mysterious cylinder of fate; his eyes were those of a
cat. He consistently won. When the others threw their
coppers on the planks before him, he reached down
with his hard hands, flicked up the coins with one of his
long fingernails, palmed them, sounded them one
against another occasionally to make sure that this one
or that one was not a dross counterfeit, and then
dropped them with ceremonious satisfaction into the
cloth purse that like a precious scrotum dangled between his thighs on a drawstring from his waistband.
It was a disgusting spectacle of rapacity. Now and then
he hummed in a thin high whine a passage from one
of the trackers' songs that only he could sing, as if to
assert, by a mere hint, his habitual dominance over
these other men of burden, and I could see their growing resentment, not of his winning, for there must always have been a winner before whose feet the con-
genital losers would be compelled to lay down their
entire tangible worth, but rather of his too evident
greed, his hypnotic plundering of their coppers. The
game broke up in an argument, after two or three of
the men hysterically accused him of having cheated.
At this the head tracker, showing a sudden contempt

for the coins that meant so much to the gamblers and until that moment had seemed so important to him, stood up still cursing the other men, stepped to the rail, unslung the purse from the blue cotton cinch of his trousers, opened its throat, and, pinching the bottom of the little loaded bag, disdainfully dropped all the money into the whispering river.

The angry talk subsided; a chill fell on the group; all were appalled—I more than any of them, I believe, for I had wanted to believe Old Pebble when he had told me that the only thing that mattered to him was friendship. Yet the other men on the junk did not seem to hold this frightful gesture against the head tracker for long; within an hour they were all merrily laughing and comradely together over some nauseating white rice brandy, called *pai-chia-erh,* and Old Pebble seemed to be regarded as the best fellow of all.

I SAT UP, looking at the view. I felt much better but pretended to be weak. Su-ling told me that the gorge we were entering had a curious name, Ox-Liver Horse-Lungs Gorge, and with a small whole hand she pointed at some stalactites, high up on the face of a cliff at the entrance door of the defile, which could be imagined to have the shapes of animal entrails; from these, she said, the unromantic place-name derived. The Old Big, as the trackers called the owner, sat on his haunches outside the door of his cabin, sucking at a hubble-bubble pipe and mostly occupied with tending it, occasionally nodding and smiling benignly at me, for he seemed satisfied with the instruction I was getting.

The morning was such as to give us pure delight. The sky was of a rich blue, softly streaked with veins of mist, so that it seemed alive, as if it were one enormous perfect over-arching petal of the universe. The mountains on either side of the river threw up red and dun and black and green masses against the blue, shapes of infinite variety, mystery, and majesty. Into the still air smoke arose in straight pale-blue shafts from tiny villages set high on the ramparts of the gorge. Here and there a plum tree or a cherry tree stood dressed in full blossom, a breathtaking immobilized explosion of color against a dark hillside. A whited pagoda, like a hand-carved object of ivory, was set on a headland at the top of the gorge. We were enveloped by sounds: the bird-world's praise of April, Old Pebble's whole-tone melodies and the boom of the trackers' drum, Su-ling's gentle murmuring laughter, the liquid music of the owner's pipe, and the endless whispered story of the Great

River's swirling waters. The cook was frying vegetables,
forward, and now and then a halo of pungent, appetiz-
ing fragrance hung about my head. I felt a marvelous,
thrilling, full-blooded keenness of the senses—not just
the quickening of life that comes with recovery from
an illness, but something more, a feeling of peaceful-
ness, well-being, and optimism.

I remember with startling vividness a few moments
from that morning, moments of a wonderful sun-bathed
clarity, in which nothing of life-changing importance
took place, but which contained, for me, as I remember
them, marvels and miracles of sight and sound and
smell.

I was watching the trackers. These laborers fascinated me, and I had the habit of sitting by the hour
observing them, while they scrambled from rock to rock
on the riverbank, straining frightfully at their halters
and dividing their heavy work evenly between them;
or while they moved slowly, step by chanted step, along
a level towing bund; or while they crept lynx-footed
along a ledge on the wall of one of the gorges, hauling
the clumsy junk against the powerful current. Their
work had a long tradition behind it, as the fluted places
on obstructing boulders proved, where tow ropes had
dragged across the rocks for so many centuries that they

had worn grooves—stone filed away by braided bamboo! The trackers, doing the work of animals, sustained their hard hours by listening to antique melodies and fantasies which the head tracker constantly sang as he, too, tugged at the top end of the towline. They marked time for his songs with a repeated unison cry at the moment when all of them together planted each footstep: "Ayah! . . . Ayah! . . ." This rhythmic work-cry had an indescribably poignant sound. The head tracker's formal title as a crewman was Noise Suppressor. With a thread of sweet song he was supposed to suppress the groan-shout that marked each painful step. He sang songs of an incongruous beauty, that were like dreams—of palaces and of roasted doves' wings and of the daughter of the mist laying her cheek and her love on a prince's pillow; while they, hauling, protested: "Ayah! . . . Ayah! . . ."

Old Pebble's voice was amazing; its range was as wide as that of the strange songs he sang—from a full-throated bass bellow to a delicate falsetto. The voice sounded the zest of the man, for delight seemed to be his main trait. His senses were obviously all at work, and he seemed to be forever on the search for new feelings, for new things to do, for new ways to lighten the endless work of his fellow men.

In those moments of which I am thinking, I was watching and listening. The cook was monotonously humming; he had been drunk the night before. On the foredeck, the bow steersman, between grunted commands to the dozen men fighting the huge flattened tree-trunk of the bow sweep which steered the junk in the twisting currents, had been loudly telling the cook stories of heroic cheaters and frauds among river pilots.

Suddenly the trackers' drum aboard the boat, just forward of the mast, uttered some kind of warning. I could feel the junk sway sluggishly. I peered over the gunwale. The trackers had halted. The tow rope seemed to be snagged on a rock under the water.

In an instant Old Pebble slipped out of his harness, stripped off his clothes, and plunged into the terrible brown water. He vanished.

"He crawls on the rocks on the bottom," Su-ling softly said to me.

I thought of him as some kind of glistening crustacean down in that turbulence. He almost seemed to belong underwater; he *was* a riverman. The water slid along. I smelled boiling vegetable oil. The trackers leaned forward on their halters. The drum kept up a steady slow beat, seeming to say: wait, wait, wait, wait, wait. . . . What was it like in those depths, for a pebble on the bottom? I was not anxious. A very long time seemed to pass. I felt the gracious warmth of the sun on my face. I was close to Su-ling. For an instant I saw a flashing shiny something at the edge of a patch of froth. The junk shuddered. The bow steersman shrieked and with a groan the men on the big sweep shoved it hard over, and the nose of the junk swung out into the stream, and the tow rope broke water with a long, sighing swish, and Old Pebble was lifted waist-high out of the water, hanging from the bamboo line; he swung along it hand over hand to the rocky beach, shouting a wild exultant melody. I felt inexpressibly happy. The cook brought a pot of tea aft to us. I looked at the magical landscape. The naked man on the rocks, sweeping the water off his skin with the flats of his hands, was shouting abuse at the bow steersman; the cook cried out from beside us, with a beaming face, that the head tracker was an unmentionable horror of a turtle. I glanced at Su-ling. Her eyes were on me, and she smiled and shrugged, as if, it seemed, to acknowledge grudgingly the marvelousness of human existence.

Was ever anyone so happy as I at that moment?

I was young then, and the world I lived in was small and easy.

I looked again at Su-ling. She was gazing at the shore.

The head tracker was already in his clothes and back on the line and was singing a tragic song. And I saw in Su-ling's eyes unmistakable signs that she loved him.

PROBABLY this discovery should not have surprised me. What did surprise me most was my own reaction to it.

I remember that the following day was rainy. The rain was misty and vague, yet penetrating and bothersome, like the murmuring of a restless crowd all around when one is caught in it and cannot move. The drizzle did not seem to fall but rather to hang about us, as if the gorge had been filled to the brim with a cool and almost weightless liquid.

I lay melancholy under the great mat arch of the fore cabinway, waiting with fierce concentration for the door of the owner's cabin, at the very stern, to open, whence, I imagined, Su-ling would finally emerge and come to tell me stories of the river.

For hour after hour the door did not open. The trackers, unfortunate creatures, were given no respite in honor of the rain; they were out in it, hauling us, and incessantly their cries, in an ambiguous heartfelt tone that might have expressed either ecstasy or agony, or both at once, came to us through the dismal air:

"Ayah! . . . Ayah! . . . ," while the head tracker wove melodies of an incongruous haunting gaiety in and out, in and out. I lay and watched the cabin door. It remained shut. I was sad. My watch had stopped running; perhaps dampness had got into it. I felt terribly lost without it, as if time no longer passed, as if the hours no longer moved without the little wheel-like thing in my pocket for them to roll along on; it seemed to me that we might be suspended forever in midmorning, like the mist drops around us in mid-air, while the trackers and the river might pull in vain against each other, so that we would be caught hanging in both time and space.

The door opened, but for a long time no one came out. Then Su-ling came out with a pot of tea.

She came straight across the wet deck to where I lay in the arched cabinway and poured me a cup with scarcely any greeting.

I said, with the helpless appeal of patient to nurse, "Stay! Sit down. Tell me about the river."

"I cannot," she said, not looking at me.

"Because of what?"

For answer she held up the teapot and poked its spout toward the cabin door, as if to signal that her husband was just then terribly thirsty for tea. I asked her again

to stay. She answered by turning away and starting
back toward the door whose openness mocked me now.
I called after her cautiously, trying to make my voice
loud enough for her to hear but not loud enough to
enter where she was about to, begging her, because
loneliness and timelessness had, frankly, made a beggar
of me, to come back when she could and talk with me.
She made no response, but passed through the open
door, and turned it into a closed door, while I became
absurdly angry at the junk's master and hers. Oh, I
hated him.

I began to be sorry for myself, and at first I used my
surroundings as scapegoat for my mood. How had I let
myself fall into such squalid circumstances? My bedroll
was infested with crawling insects, which had come to
succulent me from the hard-sinewed trackers, for their
sleeping-mats lay all around my narrow share of deck.
By night, when the procession of crawling things
headed toward the new paradise I offered them, I was
surrounded and kept awake by the tempests of the
trackers' sleeping. In their soreness they snored and
groaned, and they had active, twitching dreams, like
dogs dozing by a hearth. Some had scabby crowns, some
had sores on their legs. I itched constantly and imagined myself tainted and befouled, a piebald of ring-

worm and impetigo and white fungus. How I longed to lie in a porcelain tub in a white-tiled room, deep in the slickness of soap suds! Here instead I lay, flea-bitten, with beast-men for companions, tormented (most squalid thing of all) by want of the company of a girl who was herself, no doubt, lousy and unwashed, but who had such penetrating eyes, and such a tragic mouth, and such a mind for lyrics of the river, and such a memory for noble antiquities, in which men were brave, self-sacrificing, inexhaustibly generous, yet also cruel to death!

At last I was beginning, I suppose, to be more honest with myself. I think I had not realized in my conscious mind how deeply stirred I had been by this simple river woman in the days of my getting well, and so I had not been able, either, to foretell the effect on me of seeing in her eyes that she had lost her heart hopelessly to the singer on the towline. Of course this was why I was so uneasy and bored and angry with my lot.

As soon as all this came out openly into my mind I felt for some reason much better and I fell asleep. . . .

A gentle hand on my shoulder woke me. I rolled over into the world. Su-ling was above me. I was very happy. I thought at first it was morning. I suppose only a few minutes had passed.

"What did you want?" Su-ling asked me; I dimly felt that she seemed hurried and brusque.

"I fell asleep," I said, stretching.

"You are as soft as a bean curd," she said, squatting on the deck under the archway near me. "What did you want?"

"I wanted to talk," I said. I sat up. My boredom and disgust had made me bold, and I said, "I wanted to know about you."

"I do what I have to do," she said.

"What kind of a life do you have?" I asked with a touch of scorn.

"I do what I have to do," Su-ling said again, and there was an insistent note of pride in her repeated words.

Abruptly I asked her to tell me about Old Pebble. She looked at me for a moment, as if wondering why I had asked, then quite cheerfully and openly she began to talk about the head tracker.

He was, she said, the strongest man she had ever seen. She said there had been times, when unexpected freshets had come, when he had hauled from sunup to sundown without stopping for so much as a cup of tea.

I asked what he worked so hard *for*.

"He works for work," she said. "He loves the work for its own sake. He loves everything he does for its own sake—everything he does on the river, that is. When he is in a city he is a poor man, he is like a crippled beggar."

Su-ling told me that Old Pebble knew boats better than most people knew people. He knew more about how junks were made than most junk-builders, and he was an exquisite wright himself and had helped to build and finish and found this craft we were on. I had noticed the wonderful details of this junk—the hardwood tholepins on the stem beam, for instance, which acted as oarlocks for the great bow sweep, and which looked like parts of a piece of rare furniture, with queer tiger heads, grotesque as gargoyles, fastened to their tops; yes, Su-ling said, Old Pebble had carved them one time at Fu-ping.

Then Old Pebble had been with this junk since before it was launched?

Oh, yes, he had been in her husband's crew for many years. He was like an arm to the Old Big.

What sort of person was her husband?

"He thinks he is unlucky," she said, and she added that he was inwardly virtuous and kind, but that misfortune had made him sarcastic and suspicious. He had had a number of accidents on the river, and once he had suffered the total loss of a junk, and no one could tell him that this was the way of the Great River—that *every* captain had frequent accidents. He thought his misfortune was something special, something designed for him.

I had seen for myself that the owner was a tall, hawklike, tendinous man, with not much insulation on his wires, not the sort for jollity—apparently a dyspeptic with a talent for inflicting misfortune on himself and misery on his dear ones, a man who would charge high rates for his virtue and make his kindness felt as a sort of punishment.

I could not help asking Su-ling why she had married this man.

"My parents thought it best," she said, and I saw the sweet serious tightness at the corner of her mouth.

So it was an arranged marriage! I thought of the Old Big's absolutely uniform behavior toward Su-ling—quiet, dogmatic, and curt; while she was always submissive to him, full of murmuring laughter and approval, and ready to act on his most wantonly frivolous wish. I had seen this as innocent, daughterly affection. Now I wondered what her inner feelings really were; I was more than ever curious about whatever it was she undoubtedly felt for the head tracker, and I went back to questioning her about him.

How could a poor man like Old Pebble who had not gone to school for a morning of his life know so many beautiful songs? It seemed to me that in all our days on the river he had never sung the same song twice.

"The river is a school," Su-ling said. "The greatest scholars of Peking come to learn from the river."

Was there anything Old Pebble could not do?

"Very little," she said. "I'll tell you another thing: He can bargain. He does business for the Old Big." And she recounted how, bargaining in a boat-guild teahouse in Ichang for the cargo of this voyage, sitting at an old sleeve-polished table with his hand under a cloth clasping the hand of a seller and signaling his own offers with finger-squeezes, he had kept at the work so long, and had interrupted it so often with disgusted walkings-away and reluctant comings-back, that the merchant had at last broken into a sweat and become momentarily confused, and in that instant the cargo had been unexpectedly well bought.

This simple riverman could have been an engineer, I thought. If he had had a chance he could have learned all that I knew, and perhaps much more. But then would he have been the same man?

I asked Su-ling: Were all the Noise Suppressors on the river like this man? Could they all do almost anything?

"They are all different," she said. "Some learn from the river and some do not."

"And he has learned more than most?"

"More than most."

I do not know what stirred in me when I heard the pride in her voice as she said that. At any rate, I blurted out, "What do you feel for our Noise Suppressor?"

Again she lowered her eyes, and, "I have no right to any feelings," she demurely said.

Suddenly I was ashamed of myself for asking such a question, and I was struck by Su-ling's generosity in having talked to me as freely as she had of her circumstances. How far we had come in openness toward each other! I felt tender toward her; I wanted to show this surprising girl that I was not entirely foreign to her. But I thought of the head tracker and of what I had seen in her eyes the day before, after the towline had snagged underwater. I was, I must say, in a melancholy state of mind. I remember the strange misty rain still floating in the air outside. "Ayah! . . . Ayah! . . ." Those sad cries!

AT ABOUT this point (I remember that it was just before we reached the first of the rapids) the head tracker one noontime gave me reason to wish, and the wish soon became lively, that we could make a better pace.

Our progress was unusually slow, for there were

strong winds against us. The owner told me, as I could have observed for myself, that though storms might veer with the compass in the sky overhead, only two kinds of wind ever blew on the surface of the water in the great Yangtze gorges; there were "up-wind" and "down-wind" and no other winds, and we were getting more than our share of the contrary one. A queer thing I did observe in certain deeps of the gorges was this: However strong the gale and however open the reach, no waves ever formed on the surface in those places. All the water there had an ugly slickness, laced with froth, and the wind slid over it as if it were molten metal.

The effect of these slick places was indescribably eerie; it was as strange as if one were to stand on a hill and feel wind on his face but not on his hands.

This smoothness of the water, together with the awesome cliffs of the gorges, gave certain passages of the channel on which we rode a supernatural and malevolent atmosphere, at least in my mind.

Yet the slickness was easy enough to explain; the Yangtze's waters, I could see, moved not only seawards but also up and around and down, stirred by rocks beneath, and none of the water was ever on the surface long enough to be moved by mere wind. It fought stone, not the plastic sky. It was sheer power, and should have lifted the heart of a young engineer—but instead the sight of it made me uneasy. I began to be exaggeratedly sensitive to the creaking, twisting, shrugging, and shivering of our big junk. There was a freakishness about the power of the Great River that I did not like. We would see sudden eddies of apparently still water right in midstream, with tons of fury all around. Here and there whirlpools traveled upstream! Su-ling told me one day of a shallow near Fengtu, where, one winter at low water, centuries ago, a famous warrior placed eight rows of cairns of small stones and pebbles along the river bed, to bring about some occult military result; they were called the Stones of the Strategy of Eight Ranks. "When the spring rains fall," Su-ling said with her eyes widened, "and when the snows on the mountains have melted, and the floods come down, big trees and rocks are carried down with the current a thousand miles. The water is high on the cliffs and the noise of the pebbles rolling on the bottom is like thunder. But for hundreds of years, when the waters subsided, the small piles of stones were still there. Then one year they went away."

It seemed one could not tell what this mountain-slicing river would do.

I had known in theory how savage the river could be. In its angriest year, since records had been kept, the river had risen no less than two hundred and seventy-five feet in one of the gorges in a few weeks of springtime. In an ordinary spring, it would rise easily half that much. . . . But only now, when Su-ling talked this way and I saw how very far the flood line was above the masthead of our junk, did the threat of the Great River's potential power come home to me.

I had been making friends with the cook. This was easy. I simply told him the truth—that his food was good.

In the very first days of the trip, I had understood my status on the junk from the nature of the food that had been given me. The cook served me no meat or chicken at all, and only certain vegetables, and certain measures of rice, and I saw that the grade of my diet was far below that of the owner and his wife, below that of the head tracker, the bow steersman, the cook himself, the drummer, and other specialists, and just above that of the common trackers. Perhaps this was one reason I had fallen sick; not, I mean, of undernourishment, but of dismay at seeing such a mediocre value put upon my person. I was an American, and I had received an ad-

vanced education in the great science of engineering—
and I was ranked just a few leeks' worth above these
paupered, ignorant men.

Gradually, however, the cook relented and morsel by
morsel upgraded me. As I have said, he had made me
various broths during my illness. He and the owner's
wife seemed to reach some kind of understanding about
me, for they nodded, winked, and laughed over me, as
if I were some rare and comical taxidermist's specimen.
The cook was by turns amused and horrified by my, to
him, uncouth and barbarous habits. When he saw me
one day deposit two blasts of nasal phlegm in a square
of cloth and treasure these excreta in one of my pockets,
he actually went to the owner and complained, requesting that I be put ashore at the next port on the
river. But evidently his curiosity transcended his disgust. My diet improved, and I did not lie to the cook
about the goodness of his food.

I had got in the habit of eating forward with the
crew, because it had begun to embarrass me to be near
the owner and Su-ling during meals. Her delicacy, her
dexterity with her chopsticks, above all the motions of
her lips filled me, I am frank to say, with carnal delight,
and I could scarce keep my eyes off her face; with the
result that the owner could scarce keep his off mine.

These feasts of staring soon palled, and I sneaked forward to eat.

One noon I was sharing a meal with the head tracker, the rope handler, and a shift of trackers, and I believe the cook himself had paused to sweep a bowlful of rice into his mouth on brisk chopstick ends. Mostly the cook's eating consisted of tasting; only rice went down in bolts. The eaters, except for me, were squatting on their hams, their heels hard on the deck; I had found that my feet fell asleep in that position so popular in China, so I sat cross-legged leaning back against a big coil of bamboo rope. We were eating fried fish. We were a calm circle; the cook had mildly joked about the impoliteness of the *yang-kuei-tzŭ,* the foreign devil, me, who had not the common courtesy to compliment his hosts by an occasional graceful slurp or any other slight audible signal of relish, for he ate, the cook said, as silently as a turtle.

To this I replied that in my country only pigs' food was greeted with pigs' noises.

"What," asked the rope handler, a dull and serious-minded boy who took everything I said as an attack on China, "is wrong with pigs?"

With a startling suddenness, the head tracker emitted an angry cry, leapt to his feet, charged across perhaps

ten feet of deck, and with purple face flew at the throat
of one of the trackers. I saw the victim of this amazing
assault, a farm boy fresh-shipped on the river, who had
been the butt of much foredeck raillery because of his
greenness and clumsiness aboard, but who was willing
and hard-working—I saw him look up in a moment of
terror at his on-hurtling assailant, and he tried to let free
a shout, but the flying noose of Old Pebble's hands hit
his Adam's apple just then, and only a sickening gurgle
came out. The head tracker was shrieking curses. The
boy's head flew back and hit the deck. The other men
went on eating with a dreadful kind of caution, like that
of bystanders in the Occident at an unspeakable accident, who are so afraid of being dragged into court as
witnesses that they turn their eyes from the event with
frozen equanimity. I thought the head tracker was having a mad fit of some kind. I wanted to try to stop the
terrible thrashing but was somehow held back by the
iron hand of the others' indifference—and also possibly
by a recollection of how strong Su-ling had said the
head tracker was.

At last Old Pebble let up. The boy lay on the deck
barely conscious, moaning and rolling his eyes.

The head tracker stood up. The bow steersman, in a
quiet conversational voice, as if nothing more serious

had happened than the upsetting of a bowl of rice, asked the panting head tracker, "What did the boy do, Old Pebble?"

"Didn't you see him?" the head tracker said, raging. "He turned his fish over!"

The rope handler and two or three of the trackers clapped down their bowls and stood up.

"Bastard!"

"Turtle!"

"Idiot!"

The men were in great earnest, and they showed considerable fear. One of the trackers spat on the boy.

I saw that the owner and Su-ling had come forward.

"He took it and lifted it up and turned it over," the head tracker cried, his frenzy still at a high pitch, acting out as he shouted the motions of turning over a pan fish in a bowl with a pair of chopsticks.

There were murmuring and agitation among all the trackers.

"It's done now," the owner said in a calm voice.

"It's done, but what's done!" the head tracker screamed in fury, as if the owner had now aligned himself with the boy and deserved to have *his* throat squeezed.

"There is no way," the owner sadly said.

"There is no way! There is no way!" the cook, joining the head tracker's side, cried in mockery. "Look what's done! Look what the bastard has done!"

"The boy is a farmer," the owner said. "He did not know what he was doing."

"Now tell me," the cook sarcastically suggested, "that the boy did not know that the river is rising!"

The owner's eyes turned as if involuntarily toward the riverbank. Then he looked back squarely at the cook and said, as if accepting a dare, "I tell you that the boy did not know the river is rising."

"Then the boy has balls instead of eyes in his head," the head tracker retorted.

"The Great River rises every year," the owner said with a terrible sadness, as if this well-known disastrous fact would calm the men. "Call in the other shift to eat," he said, to put an end to the undignified debate.

It did not escape me, during these exchanges over the river's rise, that I had been wrong and blind—that these men, who had seemed so unfeeling, so indifferent, in the face of the river's awesome terrains and hinted terrors, were, after all, responsive to those things; that they were, moreover, conscious of their progress up the river, and anxious to go a little faster, for they obviously feared the rise of the waters and what might happen to them if they did not reach Wanhsien before the real freshets of spring.

I confess I reflected their anxiety; I had only to look at the floodline far overhead to feel a chill.

Still I was puzzled over the head tracker's violent reaction to the overturning of the fish, and later I asked Su-ling to explain it to me.

Pale, clearly distressed herself, she answered me in a low voice, "Capsize fish—capsize boat."

I laughed, and she looked at me in amazement and fear. It was, then, just another stupid superstition of the river. Oh, I laughed! What nonsense! It did not require a degree from a technological institute to tell that there could be no possible physical connection, no gyroscopic relationship, between the poise of the spine and ribs of a tiny pan fish and that of an eighty-ton junk. What utter nonsense! . . .

Yet how many times, as we advanced farther up the river, and as the waters rose and rose and rose, did I think of that upset fish, and of the rabid head tracker, and of the gurgling offensive boy, and of the disconcerting wisdom of some "backward" Chinese, and of fate and luck, and of the absurdity of many of my own long-cherished hopes? Yes, how often—long before we reached Wind-Box Gorge?

PART TWO

The Rapids

For several miles, as we approached the first of the bad rapids, at Hsintan, I was able to hear the dull roar of the water ahead, and I watched the owner become progressively keyed up; he walked the decks restlessly, his demeanor one of tight-stretched calm.

Many times the Old Big consulted the head tracker, as to which bank would be safer for the ascent at this time of year and at this level of water. He decided finally to use the north bank, on our right as we ascended. Soon afterward he disappeared in his cabin, where I heard him coughing often.

Out on the conning deck, that afternoon, Su-ling schooled me in more myths of the Great River, and in passing, to elaborate some point she was making about danger, she mentioned in her quiet murmur the time when her husband had lost his junk; it had been before she had married him, she said.

Her last sentence was scarce completed when the owner came bursting out of the cabin, buttoning a cotton gown in a hurry, offering to tell me about the accident.

So quietly had Su-ling been speaking that I concluded the Old Big must audit her instruction of me with an ear hard applied to a crack in the cabin door.

The owner squatted in the Chinese way and began. It had been, he said, at Kungling Rapids, just below Ox-Liver Horse-Lungs Gorge, a passage that is dangerous only at extreme low water. The whole disaster was the fault of a local rapids pilot. The Old Big spat over the rail, and a grimace seized his face, as if he were over-exerting himself by hauling on a halyard or shoving on a capstan bar; he looked as if the mere thought of a river pilot made every agonized muscle in his body go tense.

"All the rapids pilots are turtles and turtle dung," he said. "Your rapids pilot cannot do things the safe way; he has to find a new and more dangerous course each time he goes through. He wants to show the world something. The rapids are like opium for him: the more he takes, the more he needs. He dreams he is a discoverer, and he looks for new ways, and it is not *his* junk that hits the rock. Ayah, he is a turtle."

"But how," I asked, "could there be a 'new way' when Su-ling tells me that junks have hardly changed since the time of Huang-ti, and the river has changed so little?"

"There is a new way every forty years," the Old Big bitterly said. "It is an old way but it is called new. River pilots wait only for their grandfathers, who know better, to die before they claim they have found a new way."

"There are many rocks in the river," Su-ling said, "so there are many ways."

"Maybe it is worth finding a new way," I said, thinking of my dam.

"Yes, it is worth it if the junk belongs to someone else," the owner said.

In Kungling race, the owner said, the classical descending channel for junks is between Big Rock and the reef called Hsitang and, farther down, between the three rocks called the Pearls and the left shore. But here was a rapids pilot—the Old Big spat again—who thought he would find a way between Head Pearl and

Second Pearl; he would make some other man's junk dance among the whirlpools and he would be the man to have found a new way.

The pilot, it seems, had not told the Old Big beforehand that he intended to shoot the flume between the Pearls, and only after the junk had passed the foot of Big Rock, and was making fierce speed, with the trackers all on deck rowing and stamping rhythmically on the planks at a frantic rate to keep steerageway—only then did the pilot indicate by the manipulation of his fingers that the great bow sweep and stern rudder should drive the craft *away* from the shore; and the owner, standing by the mast, had, he said, believed the pilot had simply made a mistake, and he had rushed forward shouting to those manning the bow sweep to swing it back and fetch the junk into its normal course.

Not knowing whom to obey, the bow sweepers had pushed and pulled against each other, so that the indecisive junk swung into a whirlpool and broached broadside to the current and threw itself on Head Pearl and broke its back.

The junk was lost, and its cargo; twenty-three men drowned; the red lifeboats of the guild below the rapids picked only the pilot out of the water; the owner kept afloat for three long li and perched then on a rock, to be saved at dusk.

"Then it was really your fault," I had the temerity to say to the owner, "for changing the pilot's order."

"Why look for a new way when you know the old way has usually been safe?" he asked, and he was disgusted with me and went back into his cabin.

A few minutes later he thrust his head out of the cabin, and the veins stood out on his forehead, and he looked wild and furious. "You!" he said, jerking his face at me. "Listen. We can take our boat through any of the rapids on the river without a rapids pilot. We are going to take our boat through Hsintan without a pilot. Old Pebble knows more than ten river pilots. He'll take us through. You will see."

"You've been saying that at each of the rapids for years," Su-ling very softly rebuked him.

The owner ignored his wife and almost spat at me, "You will see."

All the rest of that day the owner remained in his cabin. We moored late in the evening on the upper edge of a rocky beach a few hundred yards below the last of the three rapids of Hsintan, which lay in a wide, open valley between gorges. On that spit we spent a restless night. Downgoing junkmen, having run the rap-

ids, their tension released, celebrated late and noisily
in the temporary mat sheds of wine-venders above our
beach; trying to sleep, I heard their occasional shouts,
as well as the thin whine of a Chinese two-stringed
fiddle. To my ears, which were used to the orderly
mathematics of Bach, Mozart, and Beethoven, this
Chinese music sounded like complaints against the
moon by a maddened tomcat. Nearby, in the after
cabin, I heard a constant nervous cough from the owner.
And underlying all, seeming almost to make the stony
beach beneath us vibrate, was the rumble of the river
in its own restless bed.

EARLY in the morning the head tracker and the cook
propitiated the river-guarding god.

It was not long after dawn, and the day's hard work
had not begun. The cook, having distributed bowls of
rice to the trackers and the specialists, hurried ashore
and half-ran with comical waddling steps toward the
mat sheds at the top of the spit. Remembering his errand at Ichang, I resigned myself to a wasted day—or
rather, tried to contrive good uses for an idle day, for
my attitude toward time had somewhat loosened on the
river, especially since my watch had stopped. But in a

very few minutes the cook reappeared, carrying a flame-red rooster and grinning like a bridegroom.

Everything seemed to be understood. As soon as the cook came aboard with the proud red jealous-eyed bird under his arm, the trackers disposed themselves on their haunches here and there, and conversation, though it did not cease, became subdued.

The head tracker and the cook walked with stilted, formal pace, like that of dancers, to the very bow. The head tracker seemed priest, the cook his acolyte. Old Pebble, who was unusually heavy-bearded for a Chinese, had not shaved since the start of our journey, and his whole gay head seemed to bristle with a quarter-inch stubble, all over his chin and cheeks and shorn crown. The two men moved with grotesque stateliness, each gesture a studied caricature of a gesture, their wrists twisting unnaturally, their knees slightly bent as if they were stalking something elusive. All the time they grinned at each other like a pair of practical jokers preparing a malicious hoax. The head tracker stamped his foot and clicked his tongue, to show that even ritual has rhythm. The owner and Su-ling came out of their cabin and stood at the after end of the deckhouse arch, watching. The nearby rapids roared.

Suddenly, with a magician's flourish, the cook drew

from the cotton girth that held up his trousers a short knife and handed it to the head tracker, who braced himself to take it as if it were some mighty Emperor's many-battled sword, and then giggled at his own buffoonery.

This was strange worship! The priests were laughing at the rite and at themselves; yet surely it was devoutly intended, for all were evidently in awe of the rapids and would understandably want any supernatural aid they could wangle for the ascent. Stranger yet was the god, about whom Su-ling had told me one day downriver. The river-guarding god, Chien-chiang Wang Te, was not, it seemed, a being imagined by river folk in mystery, fear, and yearning, but was in fact the apotheosis of a human rascal, the deification of a twelfth-century pirate of the Great River whose only claim to divinity, Su-ling had told me, was unending success; he could not fail in his mischievous undertakings—until, at last, meeting defeat in very old age, he plunged into the waters of Tungting Lake and drowned himself. So perhaps these roguish priests were suitable after all; and perhaps, it occurred to me, this wanton traffic on the wild rapids and in the profound gorges of the Great River *was* a kind of mischief, and perhaps it was fitting to ask success in it from a master knave.

The cook, swiftly passing his hand over the comb and hackle of the cock, fixed his broad right thumb onto the end of the bird's beak and doubled back the head until it nested on the back-feathers between the wings.

The head tracker stepped forward and, making an exaggerated face of care, slit the crimson throat.

The cook whirled and bent and aimed the pulsating spurts of blood, darker than the bird, at the top of the beam across the junk's swim-headed bow, till the arching crimson issue diminished and became a dribble and the red bundle held in the cook's firm grip let up its spasmodic struggle against the inevitable.

Then, while the cook still held the body, the head tracker tugged at a tail feather as if it were a bamboo hawser with a junk at the far end of it, and in a thin, barely audible whine hummed a snatch from a tracking song, till the feather gave way; he pasted it into the blood on the stem beam. He took others and did the same, until the whole beam was gay with two reds, of death and good luck.

The cook retired to his open-air galley and with astonishing dexterity plucked and gutted the fowl and threw it into an already boiling pot, and when the meat was done he brought helpings in a bowl and offered them to the owner, who declined, and to Su-ling, who with the same decisiveness turned the offer down, and even to me, and I was not so stupid as to accept, for I could see that some formula was being worked out. So the cook and the head tracker sat down then alone to their tender portions of graft, and washing down the sweet flesh with rice brandy at what must have been barely seven o'clock in the morning, they guffawed and got drunk over a rollicking hearty breakfast.

AFTERWARDS Su-ling came to me and said that the Old Big had decided to disembark the entire cargo of the junk and have it portaged around the rapids, and that he had ordered her to walk around and to take the foreigner, me, with her.

I was glad to hear this. I would have the pleasure of Su-ling's company all day, and I would be relieved of playing a rôle in the ascent, about which, I confess, I had been none too easy myself. I supposed that the owner's sending me ashore was more to get rid of a possible source of bad luck than to bestow security on a person of some worth.

The owner let Old Pebble take charge of everything. The head tracker was in high spirits after his breakfast, and he made a game of the unloading. All the men shouted and laughed as they worked. Old Pebble's enjoyment of the process was boundless. I was fascinated by his negotiation to hire fifty porters, each of whom, I gathered, was to get four coppers, the equivalent then of two American pennies, to carry load enough for a sturdy quadruped some three and a half rough miles around the rapids. Old Pebble stood in front of a crowd of ragbag men and boys from the village and called them out one by one. He felt obliged to discuss the qualifications of each porter, to discover each man's strength and delicacy of pace, as if the Old Big's junk nested a cargo of fine-wrought jade, and not baled cotton, to be carried up the path around danger.

From time to time the owner intervened in the morning's work, and he outdid himself with the great loudness of his voice and the darting of his eyes; he was the perfect spokesman for the anger that is the child of anxiety. He seemed dreadfully afraid of the rapids. During the unloading he danced from rock to rock like a threatened sea lion, on each perch cocking his head, gazing at the scattering of his once-compact wealth over a quarter-mile of riverbank, and then, in a quick and terror-stricken glance, forcing himself to examine the rapids ahead. He cursed his men and blasphemed against the river-guarding god. He blamed the porters for their delays and delayed them still further by the length of his sermons on their sloth. He counted the bales of his cargo over and over, and often cried out in mid-count that he had lost track of his numbers.

It was late in the morning before we were ready to leave, and off we set then in single file up a rocky path. To my distress I discovered that the owner had delegated the cook to walk along with our party and look out for the goods, including Su-ling. I should have foreseen that the cautious Old Big would take out an insurance policy, in the person of the rascally cook, to warrant his most precious chattel.

We walked at the head of the procession of overladen, singing, groaning porters up a series of terraces, climbing all the while, around a wide bay formed by a bend in the river. As we climbed away from the river on a path that wound among rocks and gorse-like shrubs, the sun, which had been behind a morning overcast, came flashing out, and the forenoon seemed suddenly a holiday for me.

Above the flood line the path moved through cultivated terraces lined with dusty cypresses, poplars, and peach trees proud with blossoms; once in a while I glanced at the river, which seemed, the farther we moved away from it and above it, increasingly benign and pure, the froth of its faraway anger sparkling under the sun like a billion of the suds of the West I missed so much in those days.

Still, though, the rapids roared.

I heard Su-ling and the cook talking and laughing, and at last she announced that they would take me to what she called the Scholar's Restaurant—an establishment, she explained, that was run by the grandson of a man who had brought acclaim to the whole province by having passed the imperial examinations in early years and had gone all the way to Peking to become a court scholar; then he had come home and had been a great official—that is to say, a man absolutely without honor. His descendants had honor and no cash; they ran an eating place. I would get a surprise there, she told me.

We walked through the hanging village of Hsintan, high on a bluff above the rapids, through shop-lined alleys that were so precipitous that they were mostly paved with stone stairs. The cook said the whole village had been built from the wreckage of junks that had come to grief in the rapids. A large crowd of gay, scabrous children pressed along beside and behind us, cheering my nose.

The restaurant was an odd heap of bamboo poles,

split-bamboo matting, cypress planks, straw-reinforced clay, and a few bricks, and it stood out from the cliff on long bamboo stilts.

The proprietor, who with folded hands and nodding head maintained the manners of a scholar in his family's tradition, but who had a very dull eye, greeted Su-ling, the cook, and me at the door with a low bow, as if we were ambassadors from a distant kingdom.

He led us first through a large tearoom near the street in which were seated the most prosperous-looking and complacent-seeming collection of men I had seen on the river. They were rapids pilots, Su-ling told me. They wore fine long gowns and black silk skullcaps, and they tucked their hands into their voluminous sleeves, and they seemed to be taciturn, stiff-necked men.

The owner took us to a small private room on the river side, containing nothing but a round table and half a dozen chairs.

The view from the glassless windows was another of the astounding, shock-like spectacles the Great River grants a stranger at every new turning. Off to the left were the ghastly riven mountains at the head of Ox-Liver Horse-Lungs Gorge, and at the right the vast, gloomy vee of the Gorge of the Military Code and Precious Blade; and between these amazing extremes, before us, as in a great bright amphitheater of a round valley, was the center of drama, the river in a frenzy.

We were looking down on the uppermost of the three rapids of Hsintan. This was made by a huge fan-shaped moraine of rocks lying athwart the river and forming, at that season of the year, a kind of low dam, in which there were several gapways, like sluices, and through these openings the water poured, that day, with terrible haste.

Waiting only for me to pay formal compliments to this staggering outlook, the cook excused himself, to return, he said, to the pack of walking rags in the street, and to go forward with them to the loading rock near the river gauge by the still water above the race.

These rapids, said Su-ling, standing at the window, had mainly been formed by a landslide in the second year of the reign of the Emperor Chia Ching of the Ming dynasty. Having been made so recently—only about three centuries ago—they were known, she said, as the New Rapids.

As we watched, three down-bound junks ran the rapids, and on the foredeck of each a river pilot stood like a black enormous bird on wide-planted feet, with arms raised and hands outspread, his huge sleeves and long gown flapping wildly in the turbulent air, but his head steady on his ramrod neck, transmitting signals to the frantic oarsmen by the lift of a finger on one hand, the folding of two fingers on the other hand, and so by sure economical movements of tiny sinews controlling the huge, awkward vessels in the fearfully entangling waters. No wonder they were such dominant, confident men as we had seen in the tearoom!

When I saw the first of them on deck there, I could not help thinking of our Old Big's expressions of contempt for all pilots on the Great River, and of his tale of his wreck, and of his boast that he would climb Hsintan without a pilot, with Old Pebble in charge.

But, Su-ling said, why had I not seen the surprising thing in this room in the Scholar's eating place?

I turned toward the girl to see what she meant, and she swept a leaf-like hand pointing at the walls. I looked round and saw that the room was entirely papered with pages from English-language textbooks, mostly of arithmetic and rhetoric. I came to life and laughed.

Su-ling told me that the present proprietor's father, aspiring to follow in *his* father's footsteps as a scholar, dreaming perhaps of striding in the robes of a great diplomat in foreign palaces, had bought these books, and others in Chinese whose pages now adorned the walls of other rooms of the house, but had found his capacities less elevated than his ambitions, had given up his studies, had set up this eating place for junk owners and river pilots, and had at last put the pages of his books to good use as wallpaper, to keep the wind from whistling through the walls of matting and uneven boards.

I began to move around sampling the pages and soon I saw that the texts had been written, not by Englishmen, but by high-minded Chinese authors, whose notions of style were grand and oddly turned. There were quaint problems in mathematics involving calculations on the abacus; there were some very strange models of English grammar.

"Why do you smile?" Su-ling asked.

"Come here and let me read you this," I said, for I had found an area of the wall that was taken up with models of correspondence, and I wanted to share my amusement with her. The text ran like this:

No. 34.

Dear sir:

Since last night it has been snowing, on which the ground is as if it were changed into a silver world and the dry leaves are as if they were decorated with white flowers.

It is one's conclusion that after snow falling the scenery of the river brightens with much more vividness.

I think it is not very prudent that we confine by the stove in spite of such a view. So I intend to get in a boat on the dangerous river for the purpose of taking a fine sight.

Though with your ability you can scarcely need my advice, yet allow me the freedom to express the strong hope that you will join me. It hurts me to consider of your staying indoors, for I regret to see you continue in those bad habits of indifference to beautiful views which may shorten your life.

> *Please write to me very fast,*
> *Your devoted servant,*

Su-ling laughed, with the sweet murmuring indulgent laughter with which I had so often heard her bless the owner of the junk, as I translated. I was very much aware that she was standing close beside me as I followed the words of the letter with an index finger, and this awareness contributed, I am sure, to the awkwardness of my translation, at which, I now realize, she was laughing, rather than at the sentiments of the letter, which were *my* source of amusement.

We laughed together. I was animated now, trying

very hard to be agreeable. We laughed, and when I had finished my absurd rendering, our eyes met, and hers sparkled, and I guess mine must have, too, and just then a man arrived with some handleless cups and a teapot. We sat down and were gay and easy.

Thus a translation of a translation brought us together, but I can see now that we were still very far apart, farther apart indeed than languages, even though we had laughed together, for our laughter was cruel, as laughter so often is. I was laughing at the awkwardness of a Chinese mind, the translator's; Su-ling at the awkwardness of a Western mind, mine. And now that I think back, I realize that the real gap between us lay in the fact that I, who was so proud of coming from the swift-winged world of science, was laughing at an old world where it was possible seriously to believe that men die young of the bad habit of failing to go out on a dangerous river to gaze at the earth when it turns overnight into silver.

LATER we stood again at the window, and we saw our junk appear next to the bank off to the left, being tracked into the approach to the lowest rapid.

Su-ling drew in her breath with surprise when she looked at the junk.

"He is going to do it," she said. "He will be in trouble with the guild."

Then I saw Old Pebble. He stood on the foredeck in a shiny black gown that had come from long repose in some boat-locker and that was much too big for him, with its sleeves folded back, showing a lining of bright blue silk, and he wore a black skullcap, and he looked like a ridiculous clown. His arms were raised. He stood motionless, perfectly poised, pretending to be a pilot. We could not see his face, but his bearing was one of contempt for the millions of hurly-burly tons of water before him. With the oversize gown flapping in the strong up-wind, even this contempt seemed, like so many of Old Pebble's moods, to be exaggerated, almost satirized.

Somehow word spread of our owner's audacity, or madness, and before long the big tearoom on the street side of the Scholar's Restaurant emptied itself, and the River Guild office across the street was vacated, and all the pilots gathered in their black gowns and black skull-caps on the steep slope between the river and the track-ing bund of the uppermost, and most hazardous, of the three rapids of Hsintan, and they stood there chattering like a flock of clerics, evidently hoping for disaster and a chance to laugh at a fool of a junk owner and a head tracker with ideas above his station.

Old Pebble stood on the deck with his neck stiffened in a manner of a river-guild pilot, his arms raised and motionless, his form utterly rigid but for the wide sleeves of his gown beating like the wings of an eagle.

AT THAT season of the year the second and third rapids of Hsintan were severe but not dangerous, and within an hour our junk, inching along close to the shore, had reached the stretch of whirling eddies above the middle race. Su-ling and I left the restaurant and went, along with quite a number of the villagers, who had apparently heard about the headstrong owner ascending without a pilot, out to the bank beside the tracking bund near where the pilots had already gathered to watch the ascent of the bad uppermost rapids.

The cook, taking the head tracker's place ashore, was supervising the laying out of the tracking lines. At the spit below the rapids early in the morning, the owner had made arrangements with the rapids-heaving concessionaire for three hundred local trackers to be taken onto the towlines at the Head Rapid, in addition to the junk's own forty-odd. This gang was now gathering.

Long lines were laid out fanwise on the wide uphill slope of the tracking bund, and, as the cook, who was perhaps still mildly drunk from his sacrificial breakfast, stamped and shouted and laughed, running here and there on his fat short legs giving instructions with such good humor that it seemed almost a travesty of pleasantness, the trackers, an even more pathetic collection of tatterdemalions than our porters of the morning, began to attach themselves resignedly to the lines. They had such sad faces!

There I observed closely for the first time the mechanism of the trackers' halters. I particularly remember this because I had occasion to think again of the fallible device of these harnesses in Wind-Box Gorge. This piece of gear consisted of a looped strap of white cotton cloth, which the tracker passed over one shoulder and across his body, and which was joined at both ends to a short length of square sennit, which in turn ran through a big stubby button of bone or wood and ended beyond in a wall knot. Each tracker owned his own harness and over his filthy rags it was his only badge of pride and honor; some of the most hope-starved beggars of all, I saw, kept their harnesses in handsome condition, with clean white straps, and with beautiful double crowns on the wall knots holding the buttons, and the buttons delicately carved. The tracker would take a half-hitch with his sennit around the bamboo towline, and when there was strain on the sennit it bore against the button and held a firm grip on the towline, but directly tension relaxed it loosened—a safety device whereby the tracker could release himself in most but, as I was in sadness to see, not all emergencies.

A black-clad pilot accosted our cook close to where Su-ling and I stood.

"What does your Noise Suppressor think he is?" the pilot contemptuously asked.

"He is an old good," our cook loyally said.

"He is an old wad of turtle dung," the pilot said.

"He has sharp eyes," the cook said, pushing forward and puffing out his chest like an urchin offering to fight. "He has good eyes and he intends to find a new way through Head Rapid that you turtles have never found."

Now I took this to be a double-edged sarcasm, directed, in the cook's mind, as I read it, against both the pilot, who could see only one side of the matter, and against the owner, who hated so bitterly the quest for a "new way."

"Ha!" the pilot cried. "He'll find a new way for a rock to make love to a boat."

"And the children of this love will be more pilots for the New Rapids—with rock heads and cypress bottoms."

"What is your owner's name?"

"He is old Yang from Wanhsien."

"I'll remember not to ship on his boat—I mean the new one he'll have to get after his Noise Suppressor wrecks this one."

Su-ling stepped forward into the conversation, saying in a positive tone, "The boat will not be wrecked. Our Noise Suppressor knows more than ten pilots."

"He knows less than one turtle," the pilot said, turning away.

Su-ling and the cook looked at each other and shrugged.

THE ROCKS between the sluices of the uppermost rapid were mostly covered. It was quite clear that the only way to ascend Head Rapid would be to climb one of the races through these gaps. There would be three parts to the task of getting through a sluice: first and worst, the junk would have to approach it through the madly choppy area where the waters from the various sluices met and mixed and fought; then it would have to go up a long, wedge-shaped tongue of swift clear slick water rushing through the gap; and at last it would have to heave over the round head of the sudden fall above this tongue and then be towed out into the apparently mill-pond stillness above the rapids. And all this, it was evi-

dent, was further complicated by the fact that there was
no sluice close against the riverbank on our side, so that
to get into one the junk would have to shear out on its
towline into the stream; furthermore, it looked to me as
if the second sluice, a good sixty or seventy feet from
shore, was much wider and more negotiable than the
first. Beyond the second sluice there was an outcropping
of dry rocks.

The lines were ready; Old Pebble waved up from the
junk. The head tracker ordered the hawsers cast off that
had held the vessel against the bank. We saw him take
his outspread stance then, and up went his neck like a
spar, till he seemed proud and ready.

"The Old Big looks sick," Su-ling said. We could see
the owner standing by the mast.

"You can't even see his face," I said.

"He's afraid," she said.

I saw a motion of Old Pebble's left hand, and fifteen
men on the bow sweep heaved it hard over. The big hull
sluggishly nosed away from the bank, and the main
towing hawser slowly lifted as it took strain from the
three-hundred-odd trackers to its point of lodgment
halfway up the mast.

All at once the junk was in the raging waters of the
approach, shearing out swiftly from shore. It heaved

and swayed and seemed beyond being steered. Above the buzzing of the pilots around us, above the rush of the rapids, we heard the dismal whining chant of the bow sweepers as they fought their great oar back toward the bank, leading the huge hull that way, too.

I heard a scream. Our cook was running down the tracking bund, shrieking like a crazy man, "No! No good! No good! The second gate! Go for the second!"

The pilots all laughed.

The junk was indeed tending toward the first of the sluices, an inhospitable little twisted tongue of water perhaps thirty feet from shore. On deck Old Pebble stood as if paralyzed, his arms upraised, doing nothing. "He's mixed up," Su-ling said in a miserable voice. He did look as if he were surprised by the circumstances in which he found himself.

"The second gate! The second gate!" the cook screamed again and again.

At the time I was quite certain that the head tracker could not hear the cook's hysterical shouts from such a distance, for the junk was right in the midst of the worst rushing of all, and Old Pebble stood stock still and seemed to be waiting for someone else to take charge.

All at once the junk began to swing broadside to the

current, and the whole craft heeled sharply to starboard, the mast swinging slowly over like a fainting man.

"Finished!" Su-ling cried. "Finished! Finished!"

The towline whipped as the mast leaned over, and the three hundred and fifty men on the bank staggered and were pulled back down the bund several steps, so that their unison pace was broken.

The pilots, who had been laughing a moment before, were now silent or softly groaned, for each could imagine himself on that tilting foredeck. Several of them cried sharply, "Ayah!"—the trackers' word, which on the pilots' lips was a shout of despair and pity.

Slowly the junk righted itself, for the towline had gone as taut as a piano string; all the trackers were leaning forward and pawing at the earth as if their own lives were at stake.

As the deck leveled itself, Old Pebble still stood there with an ashen face, with his arms still stretched over his head, his fists clenched, doing nothing.

Again the nose of the junk began to turn, and it was clear that this time the boat would broach to, and I felt sure that it would capsize.

Just then Old Pebble dropped his arms and clutched at his chest and side, and I thought for a moment he was having some kind of heart attack. But I saw that he was tearing at his great encumbering silk gown of dignity, and in a moment he had it off, and all pretense was off him, and his face had lost its bewildered look, and he ran like a common crewman for a long lizard—a bamboo pole with a hook on it.

As the junk began to heel over very slowly, Old Pebble staggered across the heaving deck, waving the lizard against the sky. He reached up and caught the towline with the hook and pulled it downwards.

He shouted something to the dozen men on the great bow sweep. They pushed down on the treetrunk that served for a handle for the huge oar, and two of them looped over it two bights of bamboo hawser which lashed it amidships with its blade out of water.

Then the men reeled like twelve drunkards to Old Pebble's side on the rearing deck and with him pulled down on the towline, and with shouts they forced it downwards until it was securely boused in a notch under the stem beam on the starboard side.

By this time the cook, seeing what Old Pebble was doing, had started running up the bund again, and with shrieks that were the best he could do for song, he gave the trackers a rhythm for their steps.

The junk righted itself. The biased leverage of the towline's new purchase pulled it around. It nosed upstream and slowly inched outward from the shore.

When the craft was at the tip of the tongue of the second sluice, Old Pebble and the bow sweepers cast off the boused line.

I glanced up at the flock of pilots. They were pale, and there was no longer a trace of derision on their faces, for they had seen an unexpected flash of courage and seamanship and command do something they could not have done in a thousand years with stately wags of their long-nailed fingers.

THOUGH the junk was now apparently safe, for it breasted the smooth, swift water of the second sluice and was no longer being thrown from side to side, the heaviest work still remained to be done. I turned to watch the trackers, for theirs was now the heavy work of making many tons of cypress go uphill on a fiercely resisting roadway of water. It was a moving sight—horribly depressing, to see more than three hundred human beings reduced to the level of work animals, blindfolded asses and oxen; yet thrilling, too, to see the irresistible force of their co-operation, for the three hundred and fifty cloth shoes of their each step up the slope were planted in the same moment, and the sad trackers' cries, "Ayah! . . . Ayah! . . . ," were sung in a great unison choir of agony and joy, and the junk did move.

It moved, however, more and more slowly, as the last and hardest test of the trackers' labor began—heaving the junk over the head of the rapid, over the round, swift crest of the sluice. The bow of the junk seemed to dig into the water there. The rope grew taut. The great crowd of towing men hung for a long time unable to move.

I saw the cook look down toward the junk, obviously at a loss what to do.

Then suddenly from midstream, from the very center of danger, came a lovely, clear, high-pitched line of song.

It was Old Pebble. I looked out and saw him standing on the deck, himself leaning as if to pull, hurling a beautiful song at the crowd on the bank.

On the proper beat the many trackers gave out a kind of growl and moved their feet forward a few inches, and the bow of the junk dug deeper into the head of the sluice. They took a second, firmer step. And a third, and a fourth.

I had never heard Old Pebble sing such a haunting melody. I saw that he was in a kind of ecstasy. His face shone in a grimace of hard work and happiness. I remembered my doubts about his credo of "simplicity," which he had recited to me in our first evening on the river, and I remembered my distress that such a sturdy young man did not avow personal goals of wealth, love, honor, and fame. Now I saw from his face that *this* was his life's goal: this instant of work, this moment's line of song, this accord with his poor fellow men, this brief spurt of useful loyalty to the cranky, skinny, half-mad owner of the junk on which he had shipped, and above all this fleeting triumph over the Great River.

At last the junk raised its head, shivered, and shot suddenly forward into the still water of the pond above the rapids.

When it was over, and the junk was pulled up to the loading platform, Old Pebble was streaming sweat, but he looked very happy.

I walked down to the river's edge to see what he would say. He jumped ashore and bent down to the river and scooped up double handfuls of the brown water and washed his face, sloshing and snorting like a small boy. I moved near him. He looked up. All he said was, "Ayah, this river is a turtle."

AFTERWARDS Su-ling and I returned to the Scholar's Restaurant.

The cook told us he would bring the owner and the

head tracker up there as soon as the junk was moored; there would not be time for reloading in the remainder of that day.

When first we sat down again, in the room overlooking the rapids, I wanted to talk about what we had just seen, and I had a feeling that Su-ling wanted to talk about it, too, but instead she began babbling about the unfortunate *fêng-shui,* or "wind-water," of the New Rapids. This was part of a pseudo-science of geomancy, which holds that the exposure of a house or a town to certain fluxes and counter-fluxes of air and moisture, above and below ground, controls the fortunes of the place, and of the people who live in it, or who pass through it, and that only the judicious placing of walls, trees, ditches, or pagodas can favorably alter them.

Su-ling said she agreed with those who felt that the uppermost of the three pagodas on the left bank at Hsin-tan was badly placed and did not sufficiently deflect the evil emanations from the Gorge of the Military Code and Precious Blade above the rapids. Many a junk had been wrecked because of the failure of that pagoda to correct the *fêng-shui* of the valley, she gravely said.

I looked at the girl mouthing this rubbish and became impatient. "Listen!" I said. "With twenty thousand dollars I could change things here so that no junk need ever be wrecked again—so that there would never be need for pilots."

The girl did not ask me how I could do this. She asked me with wide eyes where I could ever get so much money.

I pointed out to her the widest sluice in the Head Rapid, close to the opposite bank of the river, and the next widest, which was adjacent and farther out in the stream. It would be easy, I told Su-ling, for divers to set charges and blast out the nest of rocks between these two gaps with dynamite (for which I knew no Chinese word but called it "big strength powder") and make a broad, deep channel through which the water of the Great River would hurry but in which there would be no danger.

Now Su-ling looked at me with an expression of alarm, as if *I* were the victim of mad superstition. *Fêng-shui* and dynamite: I suppose they *were* irreconcilable.

"You want to change the river?" Su-ling said.

"If it makes things easier for men—why not?"

"Nothing can change the Great River!"

I scoffed at Su-ling. "It would have been much easier for Old Pebble today if the rapids had been opened up."

"Let me warn you," she said. "Never speak to Old Pebble about such changes. Never boast to *him* that you can do such things to the Great River."

"Doesn't he want to find a 'new way' either?"

"He has lived all his life on the Great River. Don't upset him. You know what fury he has in him."

I did know. I remembered his amazing attack on the farm boy for turning his fish over in his bowl. Yet I could not help laughing at Su-ling's frightened earnestness.

"I am not joking," she said, looking shocked. "I am just warning."

I took all this very lightly. How many times since then have I wished that I had heeded Su-ling's warning?

She changed the subject. She asked me whether I had heard the words of the song Old Pebble had sung while the boat was on the tongue of the rapid.

I said I had been too excited by all that was happening to hear the words.

"I want to sing it for you," she said.

"Didn't you tell me the other day that it is bad luck for one who isn't a tracker to sing a tracker's song?"

"Who believes such nonsense?" she impatiently said, who had just been talking with a straight face about *fêng-shui.* "Listen!" she said. Then, in a small, controlled voice, keeping her eyes on mine with a burning intensity, she sang the haunting, twisting melody we had heard that afternoon from the midst of the rushing rapids:

At dawn we leave Paiti in rainbow mists,
A millennium's span to Kialing we skim in a day,
From both banks the weeping of monkeys comes like a
    song:
The skiff floats by ten thousand mountains of stone.

"Is that not beautiful?" she said.

"It is," I said.

"Is it not beautiful that that song lifted our heavy boat over Head Rapid this afternoon?"

"It is," I said. "That is a beautiful thought." Then abruptly I asked her, "You love him, do you not?"

Her eyes were pathetic as she replied, "Every day on the river he shows me that life is not hard."

"What hope have you?"

"What do you mean?"

"What hope have you of happiness with Old Pebble?"

"There are many kinds of happiness," she said. "I am

happy to be near him," she softly said, and at that moment, just when she was asserting her joy, a look of deep, everlasting sadness drew down the corner of her sensitive mouth.

Then there was a commotion outside, and the scholar with the stupid face led the owner and the cook and the head tracker into our room.

Su-ling stood up and stepped toward the owner with her customary sweet obsequiousness.

"You should not have done it," she chided him, showing however the pride in him he would want to see.

"It was easy," he said. He was flushed and had evidently been drinking already.

"It was easy," the cook exultantly said. "It was only a matter of knowing which gate to go through."

The head tracker said nothing, but he smiled and his eyes sparkled.

Now Su-ling scarcely seemed to know Old Pebble. All her quiet attentions were for the owner.

By this time I had completely forgotten Su-ling's warning never to breathe to Old Pebble a word of my ideas for changing the Great River.

PART THREE

The Dam

In Witches' Mountain Gorge I began to think more often about the dam.

Of course I had had the dam on my mind, off and on, all the way up from Ichang. I had been scanning both banks every day—but I had realized from the first that on this upriver trip I could only make cursory observations, for I would have to see the whole basin, and I would have to wait until I reached Wanhsien, where the headquarters of the boatmen's guild was situated, to study charts of topography, and records of rise and fall, and data on the cities and villages that would be submerged by the lake above a dam, before I could make a more thoroughgoing survey on the downward passage. Now, however, as the days passed, and as I began to see what a dam could mean to the human beings on the boat on which I was traveling, particularly to the trackers, the dam became more important to me than it had been when I had approached it as something theoretically and technically desirable, as an abstraction in a company memorandum and in the minds of some faraway engineers.

The head tracker seemed to have been nowhere so much at home as he was in Witches' Mountain Gorge, the longest, most beautiful, and most mysterious of all the chasms of the river. This gorge, I remember, was fully twenty miles long, and at places it was no more than a hundred and fifty yards wide, and as it afforded the river's most awesome sights to this point, so also it presented some of its most arduous problems for the trackers, and these difficulties seemed to raise Old Pebble's spirits, so that for three days he sang and flew about like a wild strong bird.

The river, which in that fantastic stretch seemed not great but actually puny, had somehow during the ages cut its narrow brown way straight through vast rock mountains, which rose vertically from the water for hundreds of feet, then, falling back at knee-, hip-, and shoulder-terraces, rose again, and again, and again, all but perpendicular, until, seen through sudden clefts, they reached craggy pinnacles, like those of the Tetons, far up in the springtime sky. Sometimes the sky was cloud-streaked, and more than once we saw, back in the tallest ranges, a needle of rock piercing the underside of a layer of mist, and then, higher up, its point, visible and dry and gray in clear air above the thin plate of vapor. The rocks were limestone with overlying sandstone, and at the riverfront, where the softer rock had been washed away leaving the limestone sheer and upright, there were enormous up-and-down potholes in the faces of the cliffs, giving them weird, fluted surfaces. Caves could be seen high on the cliffs. Here and there villages clung to ledges, and sometimes these blue-gray hamlets straddled, with lovely high-arching bridges, little foaming bourns—one of which, I recall, poured out of the mouth of a cavern far up the side of a peak.

Going through Witches' Mountain Gorge gave me the feeling, as in the song Old Pebble had sung in the rapids of Hsintan, of skimming a thousand years in a day.

The water of the river itself was mostly deep and relatively quiet, but here and there, where jagged cliffs jutted boldly forward, or where heaps of detritus had been thrown out from streams on the banks, or where piles of enormous, square-cornered, house-sized blocks of sooty rock, which looked as if they had been blackened in a mountain-builder's furnace, had tumbled from the crags down into the sides of the channel—in such places there were eddies and cross-sets and whirlpools of unexpected violence. What a setting for a dam!

For the trackers, and particularly for Old Pebble, the gorge was an ever-changing challenge. The ingenuity of the head tracker was tested every hour, and he met each test with fiery joy. Here he led his towing gang over a mass of fallen boulders; next he put them aboard in a swarm, and they took up oars in erect ranks on the foredeck, sometimes pushing and sometimes pulling at the long oars, and they chanted and stamped in unison and beat up a brown froth with the wooden blades, in order that the junk might ride a cross-current to the opposite bank and there have the benefit of an upstream eddy; then for a while, shouting hoarse commands unlike any other cries of his, he would supervise his men as they stood on deck and literally clawed the junk with lizards and poles and bare hands along some sheer wetted palisades; later he would lead them on their harnesses high along a little-known ledge, or over a shoulder of rock, or across a steep scree—scrambling, singing, hurrying with elated whoops from one piece of horrible work to another. Often the head tracker was

in the sampan, sculling madly from the shore out to the
junk to consult with the bow steersman, or standing up
in the skittish boat pulling it back ashore hand over hand
on the towing hawser and roaring directions to his
trackers, who had only one guttural voice to answer his
shouts: "Ayah! . . . Ayah! . . ."

Yes, this variable work was obviously a delight to the
head tracker. Yet I saw him, more than once, in those
days, after a meal or in the early evening, altogether
composed, huddled up like a great-grandmother, with
a pensive face and a hint of easy-paced melancholy in
his eyes. I found him one evening before dark lying on
his stomach on the deck lining up a dozen peach pits,
which he had been drying for the sake of their almond-
like meat, in a row, and with a single chopstick flipping
one over the others along the row, in a kind of tiddly-
winks, and he seemed satisfied quite alone with this
game for more than an hour. Yet I found that he was
amazingly cultured, for he owned somewhat the same
rather disturbing fund of folklore and history and myth
as Su-ling; I suppose what made me persist in thinking
him simple in spite of this education was the fact that
his learning had all been acquired orally. I guess I
thought book-learning the only true enlightenment. I
remember sitting by one evening while Su-ling taught
him some lines by a poet of the T'ang dynasty, Tu Fu,

entitled *Unable to Visit Judge Wang Owing to Rain.*
Taught him? She recited the poem once, then he perfectly repeated it, and some time later, asking her if he
still had it right, pronounced it again to her without a
single mistake. His mildness was deceptive. It made him
seem nerveless and phlegmatic—until various crises
arose, such as that when, doubling as pilot, he had
tended toward the wrong sluice at New Rapids, or such
as an incident which occurred a few days later in
Witches' Mountain Gorge, when the young farmer boy
slipped and got his foot caught between two boulders;
during these crises the head tracker gave way to explo-
sions of swiftness and violent motion, which then seemed
to me mere animal reflexes, but which I now regard as
having been examples of almost perfect concord between perception and action. What could be more
civilized than that harmony? I remember now that he
was a hypochondriac, with many a quaintly expressed
anxiety about decaying muscles and shriveling tendons,
but then I saw him only as a package of wonderful
rhythmic power. He had a strange, halting grace, and I
loved to watch him fill, tamp, light, and smoke his pipe,
with its tiny brass bowl and a stem nearly three feet
long—of such a length, he once said, that he could take
a light from a passing junk.

Most of the time Old Pebble seemed kind, considerate, open, and warm. His moments of wrath, such as the one I had seen at the end of the gambling game that night, or when he had punished the farmer boy for turning over his fish, were rare, and they appeared to go against his nature. In those days, his goodness seemed to me innate, built-in, almost organic in him, like muscle tissue. It seemed not to be a matter of conscience and effort and struggling feeble heart. Only now on reflection, as I remember the signs of helplessness that lurked now and then momentarily in his eyes, do I see how hard he must have striven for virtue, and what a triumph of hard-working philosophy his simple goodness was. His life was a towpath; he was hauling himself wearily along it; his head and his heart were his stubborn trackers. He must have been trying his best, I now realize, to free himself from delusion, to struggle to rise above existence and pain, to speak truth, to be pure, to hurt no living thing, to have self-control, to have a wakeful mind, and rapturously to contemplate his short and awful life.

IN ONE day we passed the first two of the twelve peaks of Witches' Mountain, and we were deep in the gorge. The water level was rising fast. The owner was taut, and the men jumpy and fractious.

We had passed a bleak, filthy village on a narrow limestone ledge, called Peishih, which means "Back to the Rock," clinging to the cliffs like an Alpinist who has lost his nerve; then soon, not far beyond it, I remember, we saw a mountain stream in whose glen nested a tranquil evergreen grove, a picture almost too delicately composed for this rugged part of China, more like a memory-scene from a Japanese screen. Thus the sudden changes of the gorges.

The head tracker was driving his men with a relentless urgency that was spurred, I suppose, by the rise of the river. He was pressing his men perhaps too hard.

While tracking with the others over an enormous heap of fallen rock, the young farmer boy who was making his first passage as a junkman, the lackluster youth whom the head tracker had thrashed downriver because he had turned over the fish in his bowl, had the misfortune to make a misstep and to slip and wedge his ankle between two boulders, so that he gave himself great pain and, apparently thinking himself dying as he began to faint, let loose a frightful shriek. His echo, fugitive along the faces of the gorge, called pitifully back and back and back to us until it died in the distance.

Hearing the scream, Old Pebble responded with one of those seeming animal reflexes; if he thought at all of

what he was doing and would do, it must have been as
he moved.

Because of the narrowing of the stream by the heap
of rocks the current at that place was rather swift, and
the trackers were having to work fairly hard to keep
the junk moving—though this was not nearly the strain
they were to feel a few days later during certain moments in Wind-Box Gorge about which I must sooner
or later speak.

The instant Old Pebble heard the boy's fearful cry,
and long before the last reproachful echoes had faded
away, he had slipped the sennit of his harness and was
springing, with the most extraordinary elastic bounds
and foot-clipping short jumps, like grotesque stage leaps
and hops, back over the rocks alongside the fan of
trackers toward the boy, who was near the ruck of the
group. Before the head tracker could reach the boy,
the advance of the other trackers had drawn the boy's
harness tight, and his body had begun to be dragged
forward, with his foot still caught in the cleft, with a
result that, under the stimulus of stretching and re-
newed pain, he had revived and was crying out in
agony.

The drag of the boy's harness on the towline meant
that his sennit could not be slipped free.

The head tracker, leaping like a rock goat along the

way, saw this, swerved somewhat in his course, and simply bowled over the two hard-pulling trackers immediately forward of the boy on the towline. The sudden loss of their exertion had the effect at once of causing the pull of the junk to overpower the remaining trackers, and they fell back a few steps, and with their uncertain footings on the rocks some of them staggered (the two who had been knocked down were loudly cursing the head tracker), and for an instant the towline sagged, and during it Old Pebble slipped the boy's harness loose. Then swiftly he attached his own harness to the towline and started to tug, and the two abusive knockdowns got back to their feet, and with wonderful choral shouts, louder than usual, the recovered gang steadied the junk and began to tow it forward again. Once the trackers were progressing, Old Pebble cast himself off once more, went back and unwedged the weeping boy and picked him up and carried him to the water's edge, where one of the foredeckmen embarked him in the sampan and took him out to the junk to a mess of evil poultices the cook had already begun to heat up.

It was the head tracker's marvelous swift response that captured my admiration at first, his split-second solicitousness when he heard a cry of pain, his finding in mid-air, as it were, the only way to save the injured boy. But there was more to it than that. His action, which could not have been mulled over in his mind, showed a deep, instinctive love of life, a compassion, an optimism, which made me feel very good—and perhaps were among the things that got me started thinking again about the dam.

That evening on deck, however, the head tracker was for some reason extremely cruel to the farmer boy, not failing to remind him every few minutes that his injury (it was bad: his ankle was as big as his thigh) was nobody's fault but his own, for having overturned the carcass of a fish aboard a river vessel.

When, troubled by the boy's pain, I intervened and pointed out that until that afternoon the much-advertised consequence of the boy's ignorant blunder with the fish had been supposed to be disaster to the junk, not to himself, *I* became the receptacle of Old Pebble's scorn, and I wished I had not spoken, and I went aft and covered my ears to shut out the pursuing shouts.

I think that this perhaps was the crucial time: that I might have realized at that moment, had I been more sensitive, the extent of the head tracker's feelings toward me—feelings of suspicion and resentment and fear, which were so soon to catch on fire.

The boy, now useless, was put ashore the next morning with a few coppers of cash at a village called Tsingshih. What ever could have become of him?

THE DAY we got rid of the boy, during Old Pebble's time for a noon bowl of rice, I came on him mending a parrel, a small collar of bamboo rope which held the crude iron snatch-ring for the towing hawser against the mast, and which was therefore a vital bit of gear; I had seen him change parrels every day and check the ones he removed for chafing and splinters. What struck me now was the affectionate care with which he worked. He had a shell of callus on his palms, so that it was almost a wonder that he could make a fist at all: his fingers were all as thick as my thumbs—yet he drew out and replaced crushed strands of bamboo from the braid and fed in fresh lengths with the care and precision of a surgeon, and if the new strand did not lie absolutely flush with the rest, he would take it out and shave off a few delicate fibers with a tiny knife and thread the filament in again. Workmanship! All my life since then I have watched for such love of perfection in men who work with their hands. I would have lost my temper over that fussy work in no time, but the head tracker sat there repeating and repeating the same tiresome act with something that was more than patience—with what was evidently a true love for the thing he had in his hands and was shaping with his hands. He looked at the mellow golden collar as he might have looked into a woman's eyes, and as if to say, "You are the most beautiful parrel I have ever seen, and because I take good care of you, you would hold a junk in the tongue of a rapids for ten thousand running days for my sake, would you not?"

"That's good-looking," I said, pointing at the parrel, and I meant to sound admiring, but my words were taken, I guess, for condescension.

"This thing is not to look at," the head tracker, turning up his face in surprise, irritably said.

I felt that I had been misunderstood and that I must recover with a new compliment. "It's good to be able to do such fine work with your hands," I said, squatting down beside him.

The head tracker, like a small boy caught with dirty paws, thrust his hands behind him, out of my sight. "Not every man's son can be a scholar or a merchant," he said.

I was not so slow or naïve as to miss the force of that phrase "man's son," indicating that my privilege—having soft and useless hands—obviously could not be something I had earned myself.

I was stung by the contempt in this remark, and I wanted to show the head tracker that I knew a thing or two, and I thought of telling him that I could rig a bronze-and-wood pulley-block that would be a hundred times more efficient as a way of holding the towline than the primitive iron loop fastened to the parrel, and besides would not have to be repaired in many years' time. But the Chinese word for "pulley" would not come to me. I knew I had learned the word; I had actually thought of it on the junk a few days before, yet now it would not come to the service of my vanity. This frustration upset me even further, and I thought of my dam, and of what a crime it was that this man confronting me should have to spend the years of his life towing a junk up this dangerous river. I thought: we speak of *donkey* engines, *horse* power—how horrible to use the strength of men for the work of animals and motors!

"In my country," I said, "we have engines that would be able to haul your boats over the rapids."

Indeed I had forgotten Su-ling's warning.

Old Pebble was silent for a long time. Then in a tight, constrained voice he said, "Your engines cost too much. Everything costs too much in your country."

"Engines are cheaper than men."

"Foreign steamships have bad engines. They stop in the middle of rapids, and the steamships go on the rocks. This happens all the time. Your steamships are laid up for repairs three days for every one they spend on the river."

It was true; I had heard that the ships of the firm that was plying the Yangtze had had more than their share of bad luck. I felt sick at heart. I wanted to tell the head tracker that I had come to China with the idea of trying to help people like him. Yet I also felt compelled to let him know in some way that I was educated and he was not. I was casting about for something to say that would serve my double purpose—I was thinking of saying something of the waste of the farmer boy who had hurt his ankle the day before and had been cast ashore like refuse just that morning—when the head tracker lifted his face from his work with a very angry expression, and he said:

"Do you hear or not hear? This thing"—he shook the parrel in my face—"was not made to be looked at."

I was amazed by the ferocity with which he spoke these words, and I stood up. I turned away and went aft. I thought then of the word for "pulley." *Hua-lun,* pulley. A wooden block with a bronze sheave and roller bearings would be a thousand times better than an old bent iron snatch-ring on a bamboo parrel!

And what this river certainly needed was a dam!

THE RIVER had begun to wear on me, for I had had my fill of amazements and more than enough frights. To see one whirlpool thirty feet across, its center depressed nearly a foot below its rim, as if the water of the Great River were running off through some huge partially clogged drainpipe down to the cesspools of Hell—to see one such whirlpool was awe-inspiring, but to skirt the edges of a dozen of them every day for a week, as we had done, had quite another effect. The rise of the river level was now measurable from hour to hour, and we had ascended some nasty races and gone around some rough turnings; two places I remember with particular distaste were known as Small-Cat Rapids and Get-Down-from-Horse Rapids. The walls of the gorge were high; we were in a monstrous ditch of rock.

The second evening in Witches' Mountain Gorge, just after we had spar-moored for the night against a big boulder in a quiet cove, and while most of the trackers rested on their haunches on the rocks ashore, sipping tea, I sat alone on the conning deck watching blossoms of sunset unfold on the edges of the small delicate misty shrub-like clouds that stood naturalized in the visible sky over the gorge upstream—when all at once I imagined a dam.

There it was! Between those two sheer cliffs that tightened the gorge a half-mile upstream, there leaped up in my imagination a beautiful concrete straight-gravity dam which raised the upstream water five hundred feet; much of its curving span was capped by an overflow spillway controlled by drum gates and tube valve outlets, and a huge hydraulic jump apron designed to pass unprecedented volumes of water stood ready to protect both the dam and the lower countryside against the freshets of springtime. Ingenious lift-locks at either side carried junks up and down on truly hydraulic elevators. The power plant was entirely embedded in the cliffs on both sides of the river. The strength of the Great River, rushing through the diversion tunnels that had been used for the construction of the dam, and through other great tubes and shafts bored through solid rock, and finally into the whirling gills of nearly a hundred power units, created a vast hum of ten million kilowatts of light and warmth and progress flowing out through high-hanging wires over six widespread provinces. Away through pipelines flowed, too, unimaginable numbers of acre-feet of water, irrigating lands that after the harvest would feed, let me say, seventy-five million Chinese. A terrible annual flood, now making up as the river rose toward its high water level, was leashed in advance by this beautiful arc. Beyond the tall barrier, junks sailed forward with their wares, to Chungking and farther, as on a placid lake.

This picture in my mind became unbearably exciting. I had to share it. I ran forward through the mat archway of the main cabin and beyond the mast found Suling, perched on a capstan with folded legs, and the head tracker and the cook, squatting on the deck before her. They were talking in low voices.

I tried to tell them what I had seen in my mind.

They must have thought at first that I was quite mad, perhaps from fear of the Great River's churning waters. I stood there, flushed and eager-eyed, I suppose, pointing at the site and trying to build my dam again out of Chinese words and gestures, and trying to convey to them an idea of the miracles of power, irrigation, flood-control, and navigation that this lovely structure would have produced; especially of navigation, for I thought that would appeal to them. No rapids, no whirlpools, no currents, no pilots, no tracking! I was carried away and felt sure they would understand me.

The response I got was a horrifying one.

Old Pebble stood up. I was surprised to see that he was in a fury—though his anger was in check, like a line under tension belayed to a cleat.

Then I saw Su-ling look at the head tracker with an expression of great anxiety, and afterwards she turned her eyes on me in dismay, and her glance made me feel an utter fool. What had I done?

Then I remembered her warning not to speak to Old Pebble about changing the Great River. I felt hot all over.

I looked at Old Pebble again. He stood as straight and stiff as a stanchion. I expected violence.

He gave me worse than that. He turned with calm arrogance toward Su-ling and the cook and began to talk as if I had not been there in a different dialect of Chinese—Hunanese, perhaps—of which I could understand not a syllable. I had the impression he was going straight forward with the conversation the three of them had been enjoying before I had rushed in with my crazy arm-waving interruption, and it was more than an impression, it was a patent fact, that with this change of language he had simply obliterated me. I had a body, I stood on the deck, I breathed still a little hard from the thrill I had had, I was able to see him move his mouth and the others nod, laugh, and blink; but I did not exist. I was not merely foreign. I was wiped out.

THE NEXT morning there was a fog in the gorge so thick that we could barely see the rocks against which we were spar-moored. We could not think of moving until it had melted away. We were enveloped, not only in fog, but also in a profound silence. Even the rumoring of the fast-rising water seemed hushed. Then in the far distance, as I sat on the conning deck, I heard first a low throbbing, then, somewhat later and very faintly, a falsetto chant and the guttural "Ayah! . . . Ayah! . . ." of many crewmen shouting as they stood and pushed oars on the foredeck of a downgoing junk and the repeated sounds of their feet stamping all together on the deck as they lunged with each beat of the oars, and the repeated thumps of their many oars all together against the tholepins; and this pulsating noise, seeming to carry on its shoulders, as it were, the thin sad song of that junk's Noise Suppressor, grew louder and louder in the otherwise silent morning, until it seemed an almost unbearable pounding roar. It

was a terrible, fearful, tragic sound, wrapped in fog. It
was like an unendurable idea forcing itself up to recog-
nition through the murk of the lower mind. For me the
unendurable idea forcing itself upward at that moment
was that perhaps Old Pebble was right: perhaps the
Great River could not and should not be challenged by
such as I; perhaps a millennium-in-a-day was after all
not something that could be *bestowed*. . . . Suddenly,
not ten feet from our port side, a great junk like our
own loomed out of the thick morning, and I saw for a
few moments the frantic motions of the crew that went
with the sounds I had heard, and then the junk was
gone, and the noises diminished, until at last I heard
only a deep, rhythmical thumping again, and then nothing at all; absolute silence. I wondered what whips of
guilt or greed or fear could be driving a crazy owner
along the Great River in such weather. . . . And my
doubt, like the junk, was gone in the mists.

Later Su-ling came out to me and sat down to talk.
It was strange: she made no mention at all of what had
happened the previous afternoon. I kept expecting her
to reproach me, but she spoke to me in her usual way,
as a teacher, and soon the sad, fearful night-thoughts
that had troubled me after my vision of the dam and
my brush with the head tracker vanished. Su-ling

seemed more charming than she ever had to me, for the thick air of the morning hung a veil between us, a delicate gauze of moisture which seemed to smooth her hair and mollify her bright sharp eyes. She was, as she had always been toward me, amiable—wanting to teach and please; she told me stories of the mist, which is forever personified, in the lore of the Great River, as a lovely woman, a seductive princess, a girl of uncommon beauty and warmth. Where, in these poetic stories, were the vagueness, the hazard, the chill, the marrow-dampness of the fog that was actually around us, through which that solitary junk had rushed with its demonic crescendo and fading away a few minutes before?

Soon the head tracker joined us, and, to my very great surprise, he seemed casual and friendly. His manners were very good; he seemed kindly toward me. Su-ling still addressed herself to me, and much of the time Old Pebble just sat and listened, really something of an outsider in our conversation. He intruded only to suspend footnotes from Su-ling's tales, and when he spoke, with his curious rhythmic gestures and metronomic clicks of the tongue, he seemed to be trying to improve my entertainment.

Perhaps I should have thought it was queer that he

had no apparent reaction to what had happened the day before. Perhaps I should have searched his face for the too-shrewd look I had seen there on other occasions when he had lied or teased or mocked. Su-ling had soothed me; I thought the whole affair of the previous day had blown over.

For some reason, perhaps because of the rise in the level of the river during the night, one of the long bamboo spars that braced the junk offshore, while hawsers and spring lines held the craft securely in place, came loose from its footing on a rock and fell into the water. The purchase of this spar against the junk had been well aft, and so our talk on the conning deck was interrupted by a rush of crewmen to re-establish the fallen pole. As I stood and watched, Su-ling and the head tracker stayed close on either side of me; we were much jostled by the overactive repairmen.

Presently the mooring had been reset, and we three took up again our pleasant talk. Again I felt as if I were a kind of honored guest, and I was complacent.

Gradually the sun burned away the mist, and the illusion of privacy it had given me with the girl and Old Pebble slipped away, as the vague enclosure around us withdrew and we began to have glimpses of the amazing gorge.

The crew began to stir. Old Pebble went forward and beat a gong, which was not to assemble the men for work, as I thought, but was intended, Su-ling told me, to drive away once and for all the dragons of bad weather. This was the man who could not bear to listen to an engineer speak of motors and ships and pulleys which, along with my beautiful dam, would some day surely improve this treacherous highway of water!

We weighed spars and went on.

Not long afterward I discovered that my watch was no longer in my pocket. I rummaged through my gear. It was gone.

TOGETHER they had tricked me, Su-ling and the devious tracker; there was no other explanation. That jostling! That was when it had happened! I felt very bitter toward Su-ling, the memory of whose gentle instruction curdled in my mind. I sulked that morning. I could not bring myself to accuse Su-ling, and just then I dared not accuse the head tracker; I knew about "face," I knew the danger of allowing a humiliation to be explicitly seen, so I held my tongue and felt lonely and homesick. We were still in that most spectacular of gorges, but my engineering optimism had vanished, my altruism had shriveled up, and my pride stung like a slapped cheek.

Though my watch had not been working, and might never again have run, and was therefore probably useless as a watch, nevertheless I very much wanted it as property; I wanted it with a disgusting greed; I wanted it just then more than I wanted to understand or be understood.

It was mid-afternoon before Su-ling came out of the cabin on some errand that was going to hurry her forward right past me with only a nod and a hasty innocent smile, but I stopped her and asked her to chat, and she sat down as if she had plenty of time for me, and she looked at me perfectly calmly as she began some anecdote or other, and I could see the tight, sweet gather of sadness at the corner of her mouth, and I began to hear her magical soft voice instructing me.

I waited a very long time before I quietly said I would like to have my watch back.

Su-ling looked at me with big eyes and pretended not to know what I was talking about.

I repeated and insisted, being very careful to keep my voice even and low.

As to that, Su-ling said, rising and starting forward on her errand and looking at me more or less sweetly, it would be advisable for me to consult the owner of the junk; he was the custodian of everything on the junk that was lost, or misplaced, or ownerless, or in dispute. She left me.

I was furious—partly, I suppose, because I could not tell whether Su-ling was innocent. She surely seemed so. Perhaps Old Pebble had stolen the watch on his own.

I had not the inclination, as perhaps I had not the courage, to beard the owner about my watch, as Su-ling had suggested.

Instead I bottled up my anger and lay in wait for Old Pebble.

Across his mid-afternoon rice bowl I accosted him, as he squatted on the foredeck, and in a ridiculous, trembling voice, which I was obliged to keep low because other trackers were all around, I demanded the return of my watch. I had to make two or three false starts, because just as I tried to speak, the first times, the head tracker called out some instructions about hawsers, sampan, and whatnot to certain of his men. Then at last, acknowledging that he was aware of my quiet stammering over him, he turned an open, kindly face up toward mine and waited for me to speak.

I spoke, and his face turned blank.

A watch? he said. What watch? Had the young man

had a watch? What kind of watch? A watch? What had happened to the watch?

I said through clenched teeth that he knew perfectly well what watch and what had happened to the watch.

Then the head tracker asked in a loud but matter-of-fact voice, as if trying to be helpful, whether anybody had happened to steal a watch from the young foreigner.

The trackers went on eating with the good appetites of athletes. There was not a flicker of humor in any eye that I could see, but I could *feel* the mockery running around.

The head tracker told me, as if confidentially, that there was nothing but turtle dung—by which he evidently meant his trackers—on the foredeck; certainly there was no watch there. Perhaps the cook had stolen the watch.

I said that I had a very good idea who had stolen it and that I wanted it back.

The head tracker shook his head. "Then the Old Big must have stolen the watch," he gravely said. "That is hard to believe. It seems not to be like the Old Big. I have respect for the Old Big. I know nothing about a stolen watch. I did not know you had a watch. Watches belong in cities. On a junk we tell time by sunrise and sunset and getting hungry. Here on a junk we keep time in our heads. That is my whole work in life, to keep time in my head for the trackers' footsteps. I have nothing to do with watches."

I went aft, perspiring. I had lost face badly, I knew, and I was very angry with myself for having spoken a word about the theft. He had trimmed me very skillfully and made me a laughing-stock. Thenceforth, whenever there would be a burst of laughter among the trackers, forward, I would be obliged to think they were savoring over again the head tracker's handling of the angry young foreigner. Why had he stolen the watch? Was it because my watch was a threat to the timepiece in his head? Was it because my dam was a threat to his very existence?

About an hour later Su-ling, who had gone up forward for some hot tea and had stayed to talk there awhile, came back. I was alone on the conning deck. She came straight to me and in a furious whisper she said: "You foreign devil! Why did you speak about changing the river in front of him that way yesterday? I warned you!"

My anger over the watch, and my shame at having lost face, stirred me and I challenged her: "What harm was there in it? Why are you so excited about it now?"

"What harm? Old Pebble is three-quarters crazy over what you said—that's the harm."

"He did not seem the least bit crazy when he sat with us this morning, or when I talked to him not long ago at rice-time."

"He would not show you how he feels! He has been saying all kinds of wild things all day. Now he says he thinks you brought a curse on board; he says you are trying to spoil the river for us all." She no longer seemed angry with me; only afraid. "I don't know what he'll do," she miserably said.

PART FOUR

The Path

We dropped our moorings and got ready to track into Wind-Box Gorge against a swift current early in the morning under a light haze.

The river was rising very fast. While our trackers were laying out their lines, a downbound junk passed us. Its bow steersman shouted across to us that the river had risen thirty feet in three days on Goose-Tail Rock at the upper mouth of the gorge. Su-ling had told me about this great sentinel-rock, which in wintertime at low water looks, she had said, like a huge reclining tiger; in summer it vanishes under the flood waters. As she had described it, I concluded that it must have been bigger than the Sphinx of Gizeh. Now it was almost wholly submerged, and in a few days, when it would be covered, the authorities would take its disappearance as their accustomed cue to shut down river traffic altogether, until the waters would fall and the danger abate. Ours would be among the last few junks to go up.

During the readying, Old Pebble seemed to be everywhere, and he wore a scowling look but he sang snatches of song and appeared to be highly elated.

For a while he rushed about on errands of superstition. I saw him secretively burning joss paper in the cook's brazier—circlets of paper that were shiny like foil, with square holes cut in them, shapes of copper cash with which he paid tribute to venal deities. Then he hurried aft and for the first time on our journey hoisted on a pennant-halyard the owner's masthead device, which had the double use of showing that our Old Big was a Wanhsien man and of keeping off evil spirits. It was a gay rig on a light bamboo staff, consisting of a square blue flag, then above that two oblong pennants, one red, one yellow, and at the very peak a pair of wobbly metal springs, which drooped like the antennæ of a moth from the topmost point of the whole junk, and which had at their tips two tiny bells of piercingly brilliant call. All day long they poured on us their small globular sounds, like uncatchable drops of mercury. After he had hoisted the emblem, Old Pebble ran to his tiny bundle of private possessions at the head of his sleeping-mat in the crew's cabinway, fumbled in it a moment, then trotted back to the conning deck and with a comically set blank face handed Su-ling a pair of earrings which had little red glass pendants on them, and he told her to put them on "to keep the boat dry." It seemed to me that she was on the verge of weeping as she took them from him.

Old Pebble may have taken other precautions that I did not see. If his fetishes, charms, and luck-pieces could help us, we must have been hazard-proof.

Not knowing what we were going into, I inwardly ridiculed all these devices. What good, I asked myself, was the sort of bravery they gave? Later in the day, however, when the real force of the water had come home to me, I caught myself thinking angrily about my stolen watch; I must admit I wanted the comfort of it in my pocket then, as if there might have been safety in the habit of carrying that golden wafer of the hours.

The head tracker discussed the day's tactics with the owner. When their conference ended I saw the owner permit himself a rare, if perhaps partly ironical, gesture to his Noise Suppressor. To wish Old Pebble a good day's work, he brought together two clenched fists and bowed slightly to him, in the pantomime of humility and would-be servitude that a Chinese host accords a notable guest.

The head tracker snorted the required formal protest, giving it, however, a note of derision: "Don't be polite!"

Su-ling was standing by, and the head tracker turned to her, continuing his satire of manners, and said, "The fruit blossom will have her petals shaken today."

Su-ling laughed and gave back a mocking answer, "The strong branches also tremble when the petals shake."

The head tracker puckered his lips and bowed.

Now these speeches had been read broadly by the crude beggarly man and the unpolished river woman, and it had been obvious that they were making fun of an elegant tone that was far above their heads, but I saw the owner lift his eyebrows in chagrin at the highly charged words. He was as tense as he had been anywhere on the river.

A light up-wind had arisen, and in a deep bull-roar Old Pebble ordered the big lugsail hoisted, so he and his trackers would have every possible ounce of help against the fierce current of the gorge.

I was always fascinated by the seamanship of the junkmen. Their rigging and their ways of handling it, mostly thousands of years old, were in some respects as good as anything we had on our newest sailing vessels in the West. I went forward to watch the beautiful ceremony of halyards and sheets. In this Old Pebble had usually taken part as if it were a game, with open childish pleasure, jumping and shouting among the lines. Today he worked with a grave concentration. I had the bad luck to get in his way just as he was trying to clear the multiple sheets and trim them, and he turned on me with an expression far from playful and startled me by saying, "Why don't you go back where you came from?" It must have been pure chance that had made him hit on a question in those terms, which reverberated like an echo from my childhood, when I had often heard that same challenge hurled at the Poles and Italians who were coming into the valleys of my home state—and had in ignorant brutality used it myself. Perhaps he had only meant that I should go back to the afterdeck, and perhaps it had been merely a trick of translation in my head that had given his question this wider and more ominous sense. I did return to the conning deck, and did for a moment wish myself far away at home.

THEN Old Pebble was ferried ashore in the sampan, and we got under tow and entered the last gorge.

A spit at the lower end of the gorge seemed to dam up the water in a kind of reservoir above, so that within a dozen boat lengths there was a visible rise of nearly a foot in the water level. There was no turbulence. The river was simply an uphill slope. The current was alarmingly swift, and we hung fire on the sliding hill of water for nearly half an hour, moving forward literally inch by inch.

I was struck at the very outset by a new sound in Old Pebble's voice as he sang the tracking songs. There was a note of urgency in it, a kind of straining, it seemed to me, that I had not heard before. I saw that as Old Pebble worked he was forever looking this way and that, now at the slick river, now at the pale-gray mountains, now back at the junk at the end of the towline.

The owner ran forward and shouted to the drummer, commanding him to signal Old Pebble to reduce the tempo of his song, because the trackers, the Old Big cried, would need their greatest strength farther upstream and must save it here. On his way aft the owner muttered that Old Pebble knew the river; what was wrong with him this morning?

Above that first slick plane the river was violent and erratic, like a frightened thing that runs this way and that, uncertain where to make its final rush. Sometimes the trackers took a whole minute to gather strength for a new six-inch step; then suddenly the up-curve of a whirlpool would seize the junk, and for ten paces the men would actually have to hurry to keep the hawser tight. So we faltered and started and slowly persisted upstream.

I had never felt the junk shiver so hard or heard it creak so loud. All the time the tiny bells at the masthead jingled.

AT THAT phase of water in the river, fast rising toward mid-level, approaching the period of real danger, the upper and lower ends of Wind-Box Gorge were its severe passages, and between, for nearly four miles, there was a haul which was, as much of Witches' Mountain Gorge had been, awesome but not deadly fearful. Once we had budged through the lower gate, with the swift slope and then the stretch of vicious chopping currents, we went forward moderately well; which is not to say that we entirely escaped the surprises, some of them very offensive, of strong oversets, whirlpools, races, and eddies.

When we moved into this middle section of the gorge, Su-ling went into the after-cabin and fetched the wooden gaming board and the inlaid sandalwood box of "stones," and she engaged the owner in play on the conning deck; this seemed to be his opium, for he indulged in it a lot during the tense passages of the river. Having been given lessons in the game, I was permitted now to sit by and watch. Whenever the junk suffered a bad lurch or sheared away from shore or seemed stuck in the water for good, whenever we felt the most unpleasant sensations of dipping, swaying, and yawing, whenever we heard the most importunate ringing of the masthead bells, the owner rose to his feet in one of his passing furies, rushed forward, shouted as if to the cliffs and skies, and soon came back looking quite happy.

During the game, the owner talked with his wife about business matters; this was a sort of nervous habit with him. Mostly he complained in advance of bad luck he expected to have. With a really profound pessimism he catalogued the setbacks he would surely encounter.

"After this trip our Noise Suppressor is going to leave us," the owner gloomily said, among other things, to Su-ling.

"Has he told you that?" she asked. I saw a brief flicker of alarm and dismay in her eyes—but I had seen all the way up the river what skill she had in hiding her feelings; and in a moment there was no sign of what the Old Big's words had done to her.

"He has said nothing; I feel it."

"Because of what? Does he think we give him bad rice?"

"It's not that."

"Doesn't he like us?"

"He likes us," the owner said, with an unpleasant squint, bearing down harder than he needed to on the plural pronoun.

"Perhaps it is just a mood that will leave him in a few days," Su-ling said, and she looked hastily at me, and I knew what she meant—that Old Pebble would be all right as soon as I got off the junk.

"No, this is not a passing mood."

"What is it?" Su-ling asked.

"He is tired of the river. He hates the Great River."

I was so surprised to hear the owner say this, for I thought him very wrong, that I found myself blurting out some kind of contradiction.

"What do you know about the river?" he asked, turning on me.

I said, not much, but that I knew a little about people, and that I had been spending a great deal of time watching the head tracker on this trip, and that he seemed to me a rarely happy man.

Just then the junk trembled, the bells called, and instead of running forward the owner responded with a thrust of anger at me. "I hear you have mad ideas about putting a mountain into a gorge and interfering with the Great River," he said. I looked quickly at Su-ling, who must have told the owner about my idea of a dam in Witches' Mountain Gorge; she innocently regarded me, with the face of a child who remembers only virtuous acts. With a terrible scorn the junkmaster threw a question at me: "What makes you think *you* could lift a mountain?"

"In my country we have machinery . . . ," I humorlessly began, but he cut me off, addressing Su-ling.

"Our Noise Suppressor has had enough. He wants to be a farmer now. He wants to watch yellow rape blow in the wind. He wants to get wet only up to his ankles" —in rice paddies, I supposed the owner meant.

"I will be sorry to see him go," Su-ling said. It was one of the formulas over the game of "stones" that Su-ling should dully regret future losses when the Old Big confidently predicted them. Perhaps this time she had spoken her regret too feelingly; the owner looked at her sharply. She protected herself at once by seeming to be worried for the Old Big. "What will you do without him?" she asked.

The owner did not answer her but turned and spoke

to me in a suddenly gentle tone. "There comes a time," he said, "when every riverman has had enough. I, too, have been studying our Noise Suppressor on this trip. He sings badly. He wants to farm. He sings badly."

Yet at that very moment we could hear the wonderful lusty towing chant of the head tracker, and the voice was clear, fierce, defiant, manly, and, it seemed to me, full of love of life and of work and of feelings of all kinds.

"I don't know what I would do without him," the Old Big said, and he gave up a sigh that was almost a groan.

Did all the other men on the junk share this fixed idea of "enough" on the Great River? Could this belief have helped to account for the terrifying indifference all around me during those moments later that day in Wind-Box Gorge?

I WENT forward. The cook greeted me as I sat down on a coil of bamboo hawser. He was scrubbing an iron bowl, using filthy cold river water.

I asked how long he thought it would take us to get through Wind-Box Gorge.

He replied that the upper gate of the gorge would be very bad. At Goose-Tail Rock it would be very bad.

I said he had a way of responding to questions but not answering them.

He said that if we were not out of the gorge by dusk we would never get out. How could he tell how bad it would be at the upper end of the gorge? He asked me that.

"Does our Noise Suppressor want to leave this boat?" I asked.

The cook put on his roguish expression and said, "I can say this: He wants certain people to leave the boat."

Of course he meant me, and perhaps I should have rewarded him with a laugh. But I pursued my line: "Is he tired of the river?"

"Tired of the river? Does a tree get tired of growing?"

"The Old Big thinks he has had enough."

"Maybe the Old Big has had enough."

Soon Su-ling came forward from her game with the owner to tell me to look up at a cliff we were passing, high on which, in huge cracks in the solid rocks, a number of curious dark oblong box-like objects were wedged. Perhaps they were bronze or stone coffins. How had human beings lodged them there? Su-ling said they resembled the bellows of a Chinese blacksmith's forge; hence the name of the gorge.

The cook asked Su-ling what the owner would want to eat for his afternoon meal, and she said that after Wind-Box Gorge he would be hungry, that he would be able to get himself around a pullet in some soup and some fried white cabbage and some turnips; and in perfect confidence she went on with an entire menu to meet a grotesque appetite the Old Big would have when the tension of this passage was over.

The cook grunted, neither pleasantly nor angrily, at each item on her list, as if merely making a mental checkmark with his throat muscles.

Su-ling went aft.

The cook unlocked the great chest of his perishable treasures and rummaged and took out a small head of cabbage and some turnips, and he settled in a squatting position on the deck near the port scuppers and began to peel the turnips over the side.

He began humming a weird falsetto accompaniment to the head tracker's distant chant. I say weird; it was indeed. It was not so much a harmony; it was rather a kind of stitching to the other tune, a thread that was put in, drawn tight, and pulled out again, neatly and regularly.

Old Pebble's singing had an intensity now that made it very moving; it seemed to sharpen my sense of hearing.

The sampan, towing alongside the junk on the starboard hand, its bamboo painter fast on a pair of tholepins, kept bumping against the heavy half-round wales running along the side of the turreted hull. This bumping, along with the junk's heartbeat, voiced by the drum, and the tinkling of the masthead bells, and the trackers' sob-like shouts, and the cook's penetrating humming, and the creaking of tons of twisting cypress beneath us, and the hard occasional crack of the owner's raging voice, and Su-ling's soft words, and the insistent swish of the river, and above all Old Pebble's burning songs —all were mixed together in the seashell of my inner ear into a rhythmic rushing sound that came and went, a kind of panting of excitement, terror, and wonder.

THE TRACKERS climbed high across a hip of shingle and entered the beginning of a path routed by hand from the face of one of the cliffs. This seemed to me the most terrible place on the whole river.

Men working with chisels had cut out of the steep cliff a running rectangle of rock to make this path. It was scooped out of the flat face of the mountain, which was too perpendicular to permit an ordinary ledge being formed. The path had a ceiling, an inner wall, and a floor of solid rock; all it had for outer wall was peril. It ran more or less, but not exactly, on a horizontal plane; wherever possible, it followed strata of rock, presumably along the softer faults in the limestone.

I can still see vividly in my mind's eye Old Pebble entering that dangerous place.

I remember that in the gorge itself, that day, the sight gave me a sickening feeling, and now, these many years later, the memory of it still faintly does.

The cliff was sheer, rising at an angle, I would say, of more than eighty degrees; I have a distinct impression that in some places in Wind-Box Gorge parts of the mighty precipices actually overhang the river. Where it began, the path was about thirty feet above the surface of the water, so that from the deck of the junk we looked up at it, more than half the height of our mast. Su-ling told me that in winter, at low water, at what the rivermen call "zero," the path would be more than sixty feet above the surface, while late in the spring, perhaps a month after we were there, it would be nearly as much, or more, under the surface. When the melted snows of many mountains of Tibet course toward the sea, and when, riding the crests of those thaws, the run-off of spring rains that have fallen on half a million square miles of Chinese hills flow too down the Great River, its power becomes unimaginable, even to a hopeful young hydraulic engineer.

These were the very cliffs against which, in its record year, the river had climbed in a short time two hundred and seventy-five feet.

What giddied me then, and still does now, about this awful path was not just its hazardous appearance: I was most intensely disturbed by the sense it gave me of the gap between the Chinese on the junk and myself, between Su-ling and myself, between the head tracker singing his beautiful chanteys and myself, between those to whom I was supposed to provide modern wonders of engineering and myself, a putative agent of provision. To begin with, the path was more than a thousand years old, so Su-ling said: T'ang dynasty, she said, and perhaps earlier. Chinese rivermen had been satisfied for a millennium—for more than five times the whole age of my native country—to use this awful way of getting through Wind-Box Gorge. How could I, in the momentary years of my youth, have a part in persuading these people to tolerate the building of a great modern dam that would take the waters of Tibet and inner China, with their age-old furies, on its back, there to grow lax and benign? How could I span a gap of a

thousand years—a millennium in a day? These people on
the junk could be said to be living in the era between
Charlemagne and William the Conqueror, in the time
of serfs and villeins, before the Crusades, before Western printing and gunpowder, long, long before Chaucer
and Giotto and Thomas Aquinas and Dante. And they
were satisfied (or so I thought) to exist in Dark Ages,
while I lived in a time of enlightenment and was not
satisfied.

The sight of that path made me wonder whether a
dam was the right thing with which to start closing the
gap.

There was something else about the path: I could not
help feeling the incredible patience that had gone into
its making. Surely only one man at a time could have
worked there, hammering and chiseling out fragments
of stone and dropping the pieces into the river below.
How many years did these miles of jeopardous corridor
take to cut? What patience! What all-enduring patience!
And what a chasm between such patience and my hasty
world! I was a young man who grew easily bored; more
than a few weeks at any one engineering problem gave
me a feeling of stagnation, and of wasting the magic of
my youth. Suppose I had been called upon to cut stone
on a path like this for fifty years of my life, to be relieved then by my son? What if I had been called upon

to haul a junk through this path all my life? Old Pebble had this patience. The cook had been right to compare him to a tree; he endured his Sisyphus life with the same patience as a tree its growth.

Worst of all was this: The one-sided corridor cut from the cliffs was just high enough for trackers leaning forward on their halters, towing heavy weights, creeping almost; a man could not stand straight on his two feet in that space. In ten centuries this corridor had never been enlarged, but had been left the same height—a proper height for straining trackers, it seemed, not for men walking erect, proud, and unharnessed. I thought of debased men I had read about, but I could not imagine any more enslaved, more doomed, than the trackers who traversed that tight path, with a mountain of stone pressing on their shoulderblades and death off the edge to the left. Yet what a broad grin Old Pebble had used to wear at night, who had trudged through that horrible path a hundred times; what devils of happiness in his eyes sometimes!

THE STRAIN of Old Pebble's towing was great. He leaned so far forward that his hands groped and clawed along the ground. His body was leashed, but his head was free, and it moved all around, and I could see his wild excited eyes darting here and there and everywhere, searching, searching. . . .

Sometimes the hollow of the cut-out path acted as a baffle, and the trackers' shouts—"Ayah! . . . Ayah! . . ."—came down to us queerly overblown; at other times the cries were muffled, as if the sounds had fallen right into the swallowing water.

Some of the men were obviously fear-bound by the place they were in, for they cringed against the inner wall as they towed, scraping shoulders and arms along the already flesh-smoothed rock, as far from the edge as could be. I saw the eyes of some of them, gazing down on the dangerous gutter with the moody stare that sometimes covers man's terror, while the eyes of others wore no such curtains but glanced out in frank awful fear. Still others could not even dare look outward, but kept their faces turned to the beloved limestone that supported them.

Old Pebble's face showed no fear. I saw it, now and then, and it was contorted by an expression of eagerness, of yearning, of passion. His eyes restlessly roved the gorge, from mountaintop to churning flood, searching. . . .

Suddenly the wild look on Old Pebble's face made

me feel a rush of anxiety, and I felt sick at my stomach.

Could this river be dammed before such as he were ready to have it dammed?

I went aft. I kneeled by the game board, fighting my nausea. I put my hand on my watch pocket and wanted my stolen watch to be there.

Su-ling and the owner, with the sandalwood board between them, were calmly moving the wooden pips, trying with sweet mutual patience to outflank, capture, annihilate. Su-ling said to me, "Tonight we anchor at Kwei-fu. It will be dark when we get there. In the morning you will see the salt boileries. They say the place has the smell of the sea, and when we get there I want to ask you if that is true."

I was wonderfully calmed by her assurance of our arrival at a new anchorage. "Have you never been to the sea?" I asked her.

"I have been to Ichang," she said, as if she knew not where the sea might be, "and I have been to Chungking. Once I walked north from the Great River seventy-five li to visit my maternal grandmother, but when I reached her village they said she was dead. . . . Tell me: What does the sea smell like?"

"Some other time," I said, and getting unsteadily to my feet I went forward again, for though I still felt ill, I had to watch.

AGAIN I settled on the coil of bamboo rope.

I saw that Old Pebble's eyes were sweeping a cliff on the opposite side of the river, across from the tracking path. His excited gaze climbed from the water level to the very top of the cliff.

I turned toward the far side of the river. There, in a zigzag pattern up a perpendicular rock seven hundred feet high, ran a series of square holes, six inches across, I would say, and a foot or so deep. Su-ling had told me downriver about these holes, and sitting on the foredeck earlier in the day I had been looking for them. They marked the ladder of Mêng Liang, the general of the Eastern Kingdom, in the Sung dynasty, whose ships had been shut into Wind-Box Gorge and were trapped there by great chains across the river, while the army of the Western Kingdom camped in smug security on top of the mountain above; but soldiers of Mêng Liang, starting from the bottom, cut these holes with hammer and chisel, inserted beam ends in them, then, squatting on the beams that stuck straight out from the cliff, cut higher holes, until they had made a ladderway enough for a seventy-storey building, and at last a whole army climbed up the terrible exposed stairway and defeated its surprised enemy. And what had given Mêng Liang's men the patience and courage to do all this? I felt sure they had simply looked at the trackers' path cut from the stone across the way, and perhaps thought of trackers hauling junks along it; exactly as Old Pebble and his ragged companions were hauling ours these hundreds of years later.

What patience! What everlasting endurance! This patience was not simply a matter of resignation, for it had in it a large measure of determination, even of aspiration. . . .

I looked back up at Old Pebble again in the scooped-out path. He was still gazing across at the ladder holes, and there was the same look on his face of ecstasy-in-work as he had worn at the rapids of Hsintan. Perhaps he felt for a moment a tug of the aspiration I had seen in those zigzag marks on the cliff. Or perhaps the holes up the wall of the gorge, so old, so familiar, gave him a feeling of certainty that the Great River would never change.

Suddenly he broke off the chantey he had been singing, a harsh lament of a scholar who had won honors at court but had lost a love at home. For three whole groan-shouts by the others there was no song at all.

Then Old Pebble broke into the most amazing song I had ever heard from him; a whirling, spiraling, soaring sound of pure joy. It seemed to me to be wordless. He was pulling now with all his strength; he held one arm reaching forward, as if that would hurry him. Still he looked across at the marks on the reddish cliff.

His song now was like a miracle—as wonderful as the first crying of a newborn child.

The junk was tending out into the stream as it fetched around a projecting bluff, at the upper side of which the big creaking boat was suddenly taken into a nasty race of swirling water, full of froth and splashes. We were coming near the upper gate of the gorge. The water was horrible. It looked like the rushing, sucking, billowing wake of the ocean liner on which I had crossed the Pacific.

Old Pebble still stared across the river. His face had a look of great happiness or great pain—much like faces of people caught in photographs of terrible disasters, their mouths drawn by agony into seeming smiles. His song was thrilling. He strained wildly at his harness.

"Ayah! . . . Ayah! . . ."

I watched him very closely, for I wanted to try to guess what was in his mind.

Just then, at the very crest of a climbing line of wordless song, he lost his footing.

I SAW him go down. He had been pulling so hard on the towline that a slight slip of one foot was enough to throw him flat. I stood up on the pitching deck, and I believe I uttered a cry. The head tracker seemed at first not to be trying to rise. I remembered his agility in bounding over ten thousand rocks coming up the river, yet now he lay at first inert, like a man either dead or dreaming. The other trackers still strained at their ropes and still called out their slow time-beating shouts, and the cook hummed. The trackers moved forward, and the junk moved forward, inch by inch.

Suddenly the head tracker began to writhe on the stone pathway. Was he hurt?

The hands of the almost creeping second tracker had come up to the prostrate man's feet. I saw the hands grasp the leader's ankles and move them to one side, toward the river.

Old Pebble rolled and doubled up and gave out his first shriek, a terrible piercing salute to his fate, which he recognized, I guess, long before I did.

I glanced at the river. My thoughts were selfish. What would the men up there do to us? They could not slacken their efforts! I grew dizzy for a moment as I remembered the reeling of the junk that time in much easier water in Witches' Mountain Gorge when the farmer boy had caught his foot and the head tracker had knocked two other trackers off the rope; I steadied myself, grasping the mat cowling of the main cabin.

Again I looked up at the path. There was a kind of struggle going on. The head tracker seemed to be trying to slip his sennit off the towline so he could get out of the way of the trackers. They were moving forward. They were practically on him. Apparently the sennit would not relax its grip on the hawser.

Then the head tracker fell off the edge of the path, screaming as he fell. His towing harness brought him up short, and he swung there against the rock wall, some ten feet below the path and perhaps twice that much above the surface of the water.

With one more agonized unison groan, the trackers

halted. The first two men huddled against the inner wall of the pathway, bearing the weight of the head tracker and also their share of the pull of the boat.

THERE are many things about those few moments of which I am not sure, and which puzzle me. For one thing, I do not know whether the head tracker had fallen of his own choice or had been turned off the ledge by the trackers who followed him. He had been in their way; he had seemed unable to get free. I had seen the second man push aside the head tracker's legs—toward the river—in order that the second tracker and the others might keep towing, keep moving. I do not know exactly what had happened. The head tracker had been an admired and necessary man, and perhaps one who was loved, certainly not one to be, as it were, thrown away; yet his stumbling had imperiled the junk and all its crew, and all the other trackers. Who had made the choice?

In my confused reaction there was another part, too. This had to do with the owner. A few moments after the head tracker's first scream, just after his fall from the path, the owner came running forward to see what the matter was. I caught as in a camera, and still can produce from my mind's file a fogged print of it, the expression of his face when he saw what had happened: an expression of satisfaction. His haggard, money-worn face was clearly satisfied in the first instant of seeing the head tracker hanging there. Then at once the threat to his property, to the junk and its cargo, and to himself, must have struck the owner, and anxiety rushed in to jostle the first reflex aside. Close behind the owner came his wife, young and lantern-bright, and her face, too, I saw. Her first response was far from that of her husband: she was crushed by what she saw. Her sorrow must have been deep, deep; its frozen weight must have held it down; only a small part of it showed on the surface. Her response was the one I would have expected also from him, for I had thought the head tracker was a kind of helping son to him; thus the owner's reflex troubled and puzzled me.

Another factor: the cook's phlegmatic reaction. At the moment of the head tracker's first shriek, the cook had been squatting on his heels not far from me on the foredeck over the fourth cargo compartment of the junk near his open-air galley brazier; he had been peeling turnips, as I have said, and had been humming along with Old Pebble's songs. After the first cry, when I heard the Old Big rushing noisily forward to investigate and turned my head to watch him come (and perhaps, I dare say, to look for Su-ling, who was sure to be close behind him), my gaze brushed across the cook, who was still squatting, still peeling, and even still humming, though now he was, with the same precise little tune-stitches, basting not the tracker's silken music but the coarse sacking of others' screams and worried shouts. His face was placid. His eyes were on his work. Later I looked at him again, and he had still not lifted his face to the scene on the wall of the gorge. I had seen that he was friendly with the head tracker; many evenings on the river those two had entertained us all. Could the cook not bear to watch what was happening? Or was he simply not interested? Had it something to do with "enough" on the Great River? Or with grief? That humming!

Most puzzling of all: What had been in Old Pebble's mind at the moment of his fall? Had something about Mêng Liang's ladder made him think suddenly about my dam which would mean the end of all trackers? I did not know; I do not know.

I looked up at the cliff. No one seemed to have any idea what to do. The great craft shook and yawed. The bells chirped. I was afraid. The bow steersman walked calmly back to the cook's brazier and poured himself some tea. The men on the bow sweep stood silent, with hooded eyes. The cook hummed. The sampan pounded the hull.

THE OWNER began to jump up and down on the fore-deck, screaming to whichever trackers carried knives (against this very contingency, among others, I suppose) to cut the braided bamboo rope on which the head tracker was suspended and let him drown, and then tow away. I can see now that there was probably no alterna-tive to this. The effort of hoisting Old Pebble back up the towpath might have been enough, when subtracted from the effort of towing, or merely of holding the heavy junk where it was, to have allowed the current to wrest the boat from the control of the remaining trackers and carry it, without steerageway and therefore helpless, onto well-known perils downstream; and in any case, the rock towpath cut from the cliff would not have given room for leverage on the part of enough men to hoist the head tracker up again. Thus, his drowning had been de-termined by his first misstep. Dimly I think I realized this certainty at the time, though I had certainly not been prepared for it beforehand.

The owner literally danced on the foredeck, leaping

up and down and flapping his black cotton gown, like a
huge, earthbound, logy, death-excited buzzard, and he
called out in rattling accents to the trackers to cut the
fallen man away and start up again. The head tracker
swinging on the rope against the rocks protested in
harsh echoing cries. Su-ling began to whimper in tones
as soft as her usual laughter. The swift water made a
rushing sound on every hand.

At first the trackers did nothing. I was amazed at their
steadiness, holding all that wood against all that water.
For what reward? With what in their minds during that
minute? They leaned and pulled and did not move,
though the owner screamed for action.

It was at last the third man who, straining forward
all the time, slowly pulled from his cotton bellyband a
short dirk, honed on one side of the blade, and with
what seemed feeble pecking and tapping motions began
to fret the thick towing hawser at the place where it
hung over the edge of the path. He could not reach
the head tracker's sennit, which was over the side of
the cliff. His efforts seemed weak because he could
spare so little from his share of the work of braking the
junk. And could one doubt that he was reluctant? The
man who had been second on the hawser huddled
against the cliff, helping to hold the junk and bearing

Old Pebble's weight. He must have been wonderfully strong.

I will never forget that scene in those few moments—the boiling gutter of Wind-Box Gorge between fantastic vertical limestone masses nearly a thousand feet high; the head tracker hanging twenty feet above the freshet in the white cotton loop of his towing harness, screaming not so much for rescue, which he must have known to be impossible, as in protest against his certain mortality, while the forty-odd other trackers, leaderless, leaned frozen against their towing halters, straining with turgid thighs and started veins simply to hold the eighty-ton junk against the springtime river, in a slanting, rigid, silent tableau, like that of some frieze of long-ago times; the junk trembling under our feet and yawing in the flood; the owner flapping his gown and his thin beard, shouting his half of a fateful duet, ordering the others to hurry and cut away the head tracker and get on with hauling the junk out of the whispering race of the Yangtze to the town beyond; the impasse of reluctance and horror; my incredulity. . . .

I stood on the deck shocked. The cook hummed on. The owner urged speed, and Su-ling moaned with a subdued grief which seemed impersonal, timeless—the endless grief of suffering poor people in the face of disaster.

I could hear the bow steersman slurping in his teacup. I was nearly struck down by a rush of agony and anger, and of pity for the head tracker, and suddenly forgetting all my doubts about him I thought him what he had said he was, a simple good man, and I thought his fate unfair, and his companions' indifference to it seemed to me unspeakably savage, and I felt a desperate love of life, of my own life, and I watched the slow gnawing of the bamboo hawser up there. If that was a minute, it was a very long one. It made me come close to sensing the meaning of the most awesome concepts: paralysis, burial, infinity.

BY THE time I was able to move, it was already much too late. But even had I been able to act sooner, I doubt that I could have changed anything.

I ran to the Old Big and pushed him in the chest with my fists, and shouted to him to stop what was happening.

He kept right on shrieking over my shoulder, commanding the man with the knife to hurry.

I pushed and protested; he dodged and urged. I guess we did a sort of dance of death on the slapping planks of the foredeck.

Thus it happened that my back was turned when the head tracker fell into the river. I heard the brief final scream of complaint and prayer, and then there was nothing but water-sound, boat-sound, and bell-sound, and even they seemed hushed.

I spun around. I saw in the water a flash of white shoulder band. A blue-clad rump rolled over; a hand reached for the rungless sky. For a moment the strong struggling man got his head above water, but at once he was dragged frightfully under again.

"Ayah!" the remaining trackers shouted in their changeless tone. They had taken a step upriver, while the thrashing body was not yet even opposite us.

I heard the owner grunt, "Ayah!" echoing the trackers and seeming to want to add to their strength the push of his lungs, but their word was an expression in his throat of despair and weariness.

There were sounds of such strange feelings in this utterance that I could not help tearing my eyes from the rolling man in the water, now abreast of us, to the face of the owner beside me. Its deep lines were contorted; its half-veiled eyes and beard-fringed lips were terribly bitter.

What *had* gone through the mind of the Old Big, to write such changes on the crumpled parchment he wore for a face? Delight, fear, murderousness, bitterness. I shall never know; I know only that those changes hit me full and hard, and had their part in making that day one that has haunted my whole life.

As I watched, the expression of bitterness was quickly changing, firming, as when new ice spreads its brooding feathers over a lake on a wintry night.

Then this tight-stretched, rope-muscled man leapt into a surprising action—an action of utmost charity.

He ran with springy steps across the deck, and cast off the painter of the sampan from the tholepins where it had been cleated, and in his wide-sleeved black gown jumped like a side-slipping crow from the deck of the junk onto the floorboards of the small boat, which heaved and skidded away from the junk with the crash of his weight. The boat whirled quickly away from us, with the Old Big miraculously standing up in it. Su-ling gasped once and was silent thereafter.

I heard the owner shout the head tracker's name in a hoarse desperate cackle.

"Ayah! . . . Ayah! . . ." The junk was moving forward now.

I saw the owner bend down and pick up a sculling oar and straighten up, waving the T-handled blade to help keep his balance. The cup of a boat shook and

dipped and spun in the mad waters, and now the owner's face was toward us, howling the name of his head
tracker, and now we saw his back as he fought, still
standing, to keep his balance, making me think of the
mock-drunk ropewalkers I had seen in the circuses of
my boyhood.

He actually managed from time to time to dip the
oar blade in the water, in a surely futile effort to speed
his would-be merciful voyage. He went away from us
very fast. From a distance, in that haste-spoiled water,
we could not see whether the head tracker was getting
his head out any more. The owner disappeared around
a bend in the river, flapping and chopping in a regular
semaphore of his amazing balance, a tiny black staggering figure in the huge water-cut from the rock mountain,
a tiny human being way off there, erect, incredibly
brave, crying out in the echoing gorge to his needed
companion and support, whom he would save if he
could.

"AYAH! . . . Ayah! . . ."

The cook, whose humming had stopped with the fall,
and who afterwards had been standing on the deck
watching with the rest of us, gave a quiet order to the

drummer, suggesting a signal for a slightly faster pace, and reminding the drummer that the drum alone would set the trackers' rate of progress now. In this way the cook paid tribute to the absence of the head tracker's haunting chanteys, and also took command of the junk.

"Ayah! . . . Ayah! . . . Ayah! . . . Ayah! . . ."

I barely noticed how we got through the upper mouth of the gorge, for I was full of what I had seen, dazed by it, and sad.

The negotiation of that final half-mile or so—that was all, but how much!—must have called for something like a miracle from the trackers, something above heart and sinew. The men were without leadership, and they had to go through the worst stretch of the river we had yet seen. I really believe that more was required of our forty-odd men as we passed the upper limits of Wind-Box Gorge than had been asked of the three hundred fifty hired-on rag bags at the New Rapids, who leaned there on the lines but did not extend themselves, and certainly did not drain the very lees of their spirits, as our trackers must have done at the mouth of the gorge, stretching their strength beyond belief.

Yet our going through safely was not a miracle. It was a triumph of unremarkable men, a triumph of their patience and of the astounding love for each other of poverty-stricken brothers in pain and trouble.

They had eaten nothing all day. They had suffered the loss of a friend at their very feet. They had lost, too, their accustomed master, and though they may have hated the owner, and though probably none of them had seen with his eyes the Old Big's going, they must have heard his piercing cries of remorse and helpless, tottering need as the sampan rushed away from us, and they must have heard the name he called and must have known the meaning of those shouts. Now there were no more beautiful songs. Now only the hollow drum hummed to them from the junk.

Yet somehow they hauled us through.

As I say, I hardly saw any of this happen. I sat on the coil of rope thinking of Old Pebble.

I wondered again what he had been thinking about in those last moments, and whether his fall had been sheer accident or if he had been felled, as it were, by an idea, by some realization. Had he thought of the dam?

That possibility, crossing my mind for the second time, made me shudder.

Then I felt a strange revulsion and doubt. Had Old Pebble really been singing as beautifully as I had thought—or had the burning intensity of those last few minutes before his fall been in *my* mind only? Was it possible that he had been singing exactly as he had always sung, and that fear and excitement and aspiration, which I had felt on seeing the holes of Mêng Liang's ladder, had sharpened *my* senses?

What did I feel? As yet I scarcely knew. I was tired and puzzled.

Old Pebble was dead. He had been a nobody, a ragged faceless tracker among thousands of ragged faceless trackers on the Great River. His death changed nothing; there would be no obituaries. Even his closest friend, the cook, had scarcely seemed to notice his death. His body was in the river, but that did not change the river. Could the river be changed? Was Su-ling right —could *nothing* change the Great River?

Gradually, as if waking from a dream, I began to think more coherent thoughts. Of course the river could be changed. I was an engineer. I dealt with facts. Dams were made of steel and concrete. The holes in Mêng Liang's ladder were cut into hard stone. The water above a dam would one day cover many of those holes. An engineer dealt with objective facts. There was no place in my life for shadowy thoughts about faceless nobodies. Old Pebble was dead.

Yet I could not help remembering what the head tracker had told me he wanted of life: to pull on the towline, a little wine when he went ashore, a hoard of friendship. That was all. A dam was not among the things he listed. Had there been a dam he would not have died. Would he have wanted a dam if he had known that?

I am not at all sure. He wanted to haul junks, drink wine, and have friends.

I had been in a great hurry to survey this river. What did I think now about my dam—about skimming a millennium in a day?

AT SOME time—it must have been while we were still in the mouth of the gorge—I thought of Su-ling. I remembered that after the Old Big had gone out of sight down the river, Su-ling had run sobbing through the arch of the main cabin aft across the conning deck to her small home on the junk, and the owner's. Its door had slammed shut. I wanted to help her now, as she had so often helped me through uneasy times on this voyage, and I went astern and knocked on the cabin door.

There was no answer, and I knocked again, and again,

repeatedly, but the silence within held. I opened the door and walked in.

This was the first time I had been in the after-house. It was dark there. There was a tiny square opening for light and air high on the sloping transom wall opposite me. Dimly I made out two wide wooden bunks on either side, each with a reed mat spread on it. The place seemed bare and clean. I was surprised not to see Su-ling curled on one of the bunks, weeping. Her love was lost; her husband, I assumed, was also dead. Finally, as my eyes adjusted to the darkness, I saw her standing directly in front of me, with her back to me. She was gazing with wide dry eyes into a mirror that was fastened to a stanchion, with the meager light from the little window on her face.

Becoming aware of me, she turned and brushed past me and walked out onto the conning deck. Her face was the one she always showed, unfurrowed, sweet, and bright, with only the tuck of everlasting woe at the corner of her mouth to show for the day's catastrophes. She did not look at me. Her hands worked at one earlobe as she walked, then at the other, and following her I saw her go to the port side, facing the open river, and there she threw the red earrings Old Pebble had given her into the man-eating water.

She wheeled and went quickly back into the cabin. I did not go in after her, because it was clear that she wanted to be alone.

The door closed, and then, within, I heard deep muffled sobs from this river girl who did her best to hide her feelings from the world.

OF OUR getting out of the gorge, I remember only one sight that makes me realize how fierce the effort of the trackers must have been—the sight of the great sentinel-rock at the very gate, against the upper face of which the rushing river was smoothly mounded up, as water is piled in a hill around the prow of a blunt swift-moving cargo vessel.

At length we somehow reached the placid open valley above the gorge. The river was wide there, and calm, like a slowly moving lake, if such a thing could be. The surcease from quaking and rocking, and the sudden total lifting of danger, gave me a queer feeling of being suddenly sleepy, drugged, let wholly down into good darkness. One would have thought the trackers' cries should have been triumphant here, for surely they had overreached their known powers, and they had passed out of the gate of the last of the gorges, and they must have felt themselves great men in their line, and close friends; but their groan-shout was unchanged, and it had the selfsame sound of the trackers' cry which had not changed for two or three thousand years, half agony, half exultation, a patient measuring of steps in time and space: "Ayah! . . . Ayah! . . ."

It was dark by the time we anchored for the night, off the banks of Kweifu. The cook divided the enormous supper he had prepared for the owner among the bowls of the trackers, who would otherwise have received that night, as every other night, rations of rice palliated with a few snippets of fried cabbage. They ate bolting like curs and lay down and slept at once.

The cook cleaned his pots by lantern light. Then he bundled up his belongings and carried them aft with the lantern and moved into the owner's cabin, from which Su-ling's helpless sobs still came. I lay in my bedroll so taken up with all I had seen and felt that day that I was not even surprised or angered by this invasion of the cook's. The trackers moaned in their sleep— the only mourning I ever heard them give Old Pebble, who had once told me he would surely have a fine funeral, bought with the coppers of friendship. I could see through the cracks in the cabin wall that the lantern shone within. Late at night I still heard Su-ling's weeping, and over it I heard the clicking of an abacus, as the cook, in his new rôle as commander of the junk, made calculations of wages and probable sales and possible profits.

I WAS up very early the next morning, as it was barely getting light. Some distance from our anchorage, I saw the salt wells of Kweifu, where, though the rise of the river had brought the season of work almost to an end, the scores of massive half-buried caldrons along the riverbank were still being fired day and night and were all boiling. From our viewpoint, when the first pink rays of sunlight slanted through the gate of the gorges onto the field of steam, it looked as if the vapors of a still-hot inner earth were escaping to the regions of man.

The cook had to go ashore to buy a sampan, and I went with him, to see the wells; we disembarked onto a shelf of shale by a long plank.

At the wells I was greeted by the sight of hundreds of naked men toiling up and down the spiral interior paths of the enormous brine pits. I began at first, seeing these figures that reminded me of Blake and Dante and Milton, to feel some kind of shallow theoretical distress, over men like these who were forced to do the work, not merely of animals, but of the most primitive machines, and this tripped off, as it made me think first of our trackers, then sharply of Old Pebble, and of the harrowing previous day, an overwhelming emotion of personal loss, and a very strong feeling of waste; cringing back from the brink of one of the huge conical pits, I was overcome by a sudden rage.

Later, back on the junk, as we moved on upriver, trying to purge myself of some of this anger, which lingered on, I tried to tell the cook that I knew of a well-known brand of submersible pump, which looked like a diving-bell, that could have been bought for no more, surely, than a month's wages for all the well-slaves of Kweifu and that alone would do the work of all those men, and would free them.

The cook dismissed me and my pump by saying that our salt wouldn't taste good.

I bit my lip and turned to Su-ling and said with a sad heart that the sea had a different smell from that of the brine pits; the pits smelled only of bitter salt, of tears and sweat, while the sea smells of the sun and spindrift and seaweed and voyages and living things. . . . But Su-ling only stared, unhearing.

We were all moody that day. We were out of the gorge; it was an easy day on the river. We made twenty miles. We were all quiet.

Some of the crew came to the cook in the evening and asked him to get out paper and brush and ink block and write a letter for them to the Emperor of the Dead at Fengtu, requesting a passport for their head tracker to that place where all good junkmen go.

The cook was disgusted; he said that this was a silly thing to do. All the same, he wrote the letter and gave it to the men, and they put it into the celestial post— which is to say, they burned it in the cook's charcoal brazier.

Condescendingly the cook said to me, "Ignorant men!" I thought of the day at the New Rapids when he and the head tracker had sacrificed the cock at the stem beam; of his look then of half-trust, half-belief.

I asked the cook why no one ever spoke of the owner.

He said the owner was not dead; he would be back.

I asked how he could know that.

He replied that the owner, one of the best boatmen on the river, had been in a boat, and he was surely alive and would come back; whereas Old Pebble, one of the best trackers on the river, had been *in* the river, and, he said, "The river when it is rising never gives back a life."

If the request for a passport from the Emperor of the Dead was absurd, where, then, I asked, was the head tracker's soul; what had become of the spirit that had

made the songs of work so incredibly happy? Where
was it now? Where would it go?

The cook looked across the gunwale at the dark river
away from me and slowly asked, "Where does the flame
go when we put a fire out?"

IT TOOK us three days to reach Wanhsien. The cook
had discussed with Su-ling whether we should lie idle
somewhere and wait for the owner, who, they both felt
sure, would catch a ride up the river on another man's
junk; they decided, in view of the ever-rising waters, to
go on, and after three days, moving through foothills
on a swift but not dangerous river, we came during a
sunset hour to our destination.

We passed a pagoda of thirteen storeys and then, at
a great elbow in the river, arrived at the city of Wanhsien. We moored on the opposite bank.

We saw across the way a city built on a hill among
hills. On the far horizon were high mountains, their
rock foreheads red in the evening light, and below
them were darker ranges of flat-topped hills, which in
the faint low-lying mists of evening seemed a series of
long cardboard cut-outs standing in the mysterious soft
thick whitish-purple air, one in front of the other; and

nearer still were terraced hills luxuriant with precious tung trees, layered early wheat, and rape and barley and beans, and poppies in a mist-softened clamor of bloom.

All these hills embraced the loud hill of the city, which, capped with a teeming architecture above the flood line, was widely split, directly across from us, by an amazing stairway. The stone stairs must have been twice as wide as the great boulevards of Western cities, and they rose and rose and rose from the surface of the river to the very crown of the life on the heights; at any level of the Great River, sampans could touch at the stairs and their passengers could alight with a sense of the hospitality of the place and go up to its turmoil with a certain amount of dignity.

We tied up in a forest of masts across the water, amid shouting and a bustle that was as dazzling and depressing, in its different way, as the churning waters of the lonely river had been.

Here was a terminal of commerce, a big shifting-place of rice and salt and coal and cotton and tree oil and paper made from bamboo, and many other wanted things, and the greeds and lusts and bitternesses of the floating market were noisy and confusing, after the weeks of the spare, melancholy sounds of our progress up the river.

Up from the city across from us, besides, drifted a cloud of the sounds of humanity: hawking, screams of laughter, the claims of beggars on their fellow men, the kitten-cry of infants, venders' drums, the noise of bells and fiddles, the chants of magicians and jugglers, the moaning and intonations of priests and religious maniacs, and the underlying murmur of gossip, games, neighborly argument, story-telling, love-making—of all kinds of evening solace for hard daytime toil.

I did not want to leave the junk to go into that noisy town, but I knew I must. The cook told me the name of an inn on a street on the brow of the town that was suitable, he said with a pucker of his lips that expressed some kind of irony, for junk owners and foreigners. I packed my Gladstone bag and then stood on deck while a young tracker was sent to fetch a taxi-sampan that would ferry me across the river.

As I waited I had an inspiration, to put off the heavy feeling of impending loneliness that oppressed me: Su-ling and the cook and the bow steersman and the helmsman and the drummer and the rope coiler—all the specialists, about a dozen boatmen—must come to the inn and be my guests at a banquet of farewell that evening.

The cook and Su-ling demurred; they said they wanted the honor of entertaining me, but I could see

that their protests were ceremonial, and we soon settled
the matter in my favor.

I had a melancholy sense of the finality of this parting
from the junk, but when I feelingly called, "Until again!"
to the trackers, to those ragged wonders who had
brought us through the gate of Wind-Box Gorge and
who now sat apathetic under their mat shed, lice-picking, snoozing, staring, too poor to go ashore and cele-
brate their little victory over time and space and the
river—too familiar, perhaps, with unending pain and
work and loss and aches even to have seen it as a victory;
when I called a heartfelt informal farewell to them, I
say, only two or three looked up at me, and those gaped
at me as if I were a total stranger, and did not even
grunt a reply but went back to their trivial concerns.

The sampan came by, with two rowers, and already
loaded with nearly a dozen passengers, and a mound of
their goods, so that the light boat had only a few inches
of freeboard and might easily be overturned, yet I had
no choice but to pack myself and my bag aboard, and
we pulled away from the junk, and when we were fifty
feet away I could not tell the vessel on which I had lived
for all those days from the others with which it was tied
in a crowd of sameness. The junks were all alike. Could
each of them have had a trip upriver like ours? And

could this have been going on for three or four thousand years?

Our boatmen poled us far upstream in the quiet shallow water along the bank, then, a mile above the city, they dropped their poles, took up oars, and rowed out into the swift current with all their strength. We went diagonally across and down toward the wide stairs of the city. With each push of the oars the ferrymen stamped their feet and gave out a kind of grunt, a rudimentary "Ayah! . . ."

When I heard that sound I was overwhelmed with emotion. The scene in Wind-Box Gorge leaped vividly into my mind, and I closed my eyes and saw again the disturbing trifles—the Old Big's expression, the blank face of the humming cook, the hesitant third tracker pecking at the hawser with his knife, Su-ling in true despair, the bow steersman slaking his thirst at the teapot, and the doomed head tracker himself thrashing at the end of the rope—and the water; the froth and waves of the Great River. Then in that unstable sampan, in mid-current, I felt the beginnings of something I had never experienced before at that age, a feeling very deep that I would have found hard then to define— something close to anger, yet close as well to love, a feeling in which pain and joy were mixed; something like determination; perhaps the very first stirring of understanding in me, though I was terribly troubled still by the many things I did not understand. This strange new feeling was, at any rate, more a physical sensation than anything else in those first moments, an upsurge in my chest of elation-with-despair, of a palpable ache that somehow gave me comfort. I know now, for I have experienced it often, that this feeling was really a kind of wishing—that things could be different, that I could be a better person, that the world could be a better place; and with the wishing, a feeling of sadness, regret, and even, it may be, of hopelessness. Many of my friends say they have had this feeling, too; it seems to be a common sensation of our anxious era, which rushes along as swiftly as the Great River in flood. The feeling quickly passed that time, supplanted by a rush of the misery of parting—of leave-taking from a place that demanded awe, from an experience I could never forget, and from human beings whom I had come close to understanding.

Our ferrymen made their landfall, after ten minutes of hard work, at the very center of the stone stairway to the city. They charged me three times as much as any of the Chinese aboard, and for a few moments I was very angry. I remember that during my brief altercation with the ferrymen I absent-mindedly patted the watch pocket in my trousers and was spurred to new heights of pettiness, contempt, and frustrating anger by a sharp thought of my golden timepiece stolen on the junk.

The ferrymen shouted loudly at me and made me appear to be a robber and oppressor for balking at paying them only three times the normal fare, and a crowd gathered, and I was soon very much out of sorts.

I paid off the ferrymen and asked my way to the inn.

The whole noisy crowd offered to lead the way, and we set off in a human wave up the stairway. Beggars pressed around me, touching my arms and whispering their needs. Friendly men offered to carry my bag, but thievery and high rates were in my mind, and I clutched the handle ever more fiercely. We flowed up to the crest of the city, gathering new adherents all the way.

At last we came to the inn. The door was locked. One of my most aggressive bodyguards, a grinning hunched-over lad with a great white fungus scab-cap on his shaven crown, pulled the handle of the doorbell, and far away, above the noise of my personal crowd, I heard a tiny ringing—and again was stirred by strong feelings, as I thought of the tinkling of the masthead bells in the gorge.

Soon a white-bearded man dressed in a silk gown appeared at the door, and he bowed to me; then he darted inside for a moment and reappeared with a bamboo staff and began screaming at my followers and flailing about with the dangerous rod. The crowd fell back, cursing and laughing, but did not adjourn.

How grand it made me feel, I confess, to have been greeted by a man clothed in silk!

The man, who turned out to be a brother of the innkeeper, pushed me inside the door and quickly bolted it. One could hear the crowd suddenly murmur and melt.

I negotiated for a room, ordered several dishes for my modest banquet, and then at once asked for a bath.

In a dark, damp, moldy-smelling cavern at the back of the inn I was presently squatting shoulder-deep in a round wooden tub of painfully hot water, and I stayed in it, lathering, rinsing, and growing happier and happier, till it was tepid. Then I put on clean clothes from my bag. I lay down on the brick bed in my whitewashed room to wait for my guests. I felt like a new person. I even began to think back through the gorges in quest of the memory of a suitable dam site.

FROM the moment the innkeeper's brother came bursting into my room to tell me that there were some "river people" at the gate asking for me, I knew that my idea of having a banquet had been a mistake. He looked ill of a bad smell.

I walked with him out into the front courtyard of the inn, and soon I stood with Su-ling and the cook and the others in a reception parlor and stared at them, grotesque in their dirty quilted cotton clothes beside the graceful city man in his silken gown, who looked thunderstruck at the news that *these* were the foreigner's guests, and my heart sank.

Su-ling stood at a disadvantage before a delicate Coromandel screen; her wrists looked thick, and greasy strings of hair dangled over her cheek. The boatmen glanced around with wide, unsophisticated eyes. They talked and laughed very loudly. I yearned for my now lost illusion of the simple beauty my friends had seemed to have at home on the junk.

We sat at a table in a private room. The boatmen ate noisily. Su-ling beside me spoke not a word and ate little.

I ordered a bottle of rice wine and would have started some toasts, in an effort to break our sad reserve, but not having experienced the local way of exchanging toasts, man to man, I proposed a general drinking, to the Great River. The junkmen did not understand my intention, and they stared rather fearfully at me, as if

I had uttered some kind of curse. The cook eventually found the means of drinking more than his share of the bottle.

Later in the difficult meal I blurted out a question. Could not Old Pebble have been spared?

"Finished," the half-drunk cook said. "He was finished."

Was it simply, then, that Old Pebble had done the work of his days and was exhausted, his heart spent? Was it simply that he had come to his time of "enough" on the Great River? I was an engineer; this concept angered me. "There should have been some way to save him," I said.

"Ayah, he was greedy," the cook said, with a hateful expression. "He wanted to own the junk. He wanted to be in charge of everybody."

I shrugged my shoulders. I thought the cook was really talking about himself. I tried to get some comment from Su-ling, but her eyes remained fixed on her nearly full plate, and she was silent.

The teapot went around and around the table, but we never attained anything like ease.

Then there was a fuss in the inn, and the owner of our junk rushed into our room. He was even filthier than the rest of his people, and he looked terribly gaunt and soul-burnt; his stringy muscles all seemed knotted and stretched, and his eyes were fierce within reddened lids.

I saw the cook's face fall in an almost comical way when he saw the Old Big, even though he had declared himself certain that the owner would rejoin us.

The owner was in a rage. What was the idea of leaving the junk, fully loaded, in the power of a handful of turtles? What were his specialists doing in *this* place?

I tried to ask him to sit down and join us.

He ignored me. He shouted to the cook that the junk was moored in a very bad place, that unloading from that place would be impossible; the junk would have to be moved; they must all come away at once and move the junk to a place nearer the tax scales.

I asked as firmly as I could what news there was of Old Pebble.

"No way, no way," the owner irritably said.

Then he turned on the cook and asked with a cracking voice what the meaning was of the cook's having moved his possessions into the after-cabin.

The boatmen were mostly standing now. Su-ling got up. I saw that our little party was over, and I felt very unhappy.

In a somewhat secretive way I murmured to Su-ling my thanks for all she had taught me.

"Don't be polite," she casually said. I sought in her eyes some sign of deeper feeling than her tossing out of this formula had contained, but she turned away and looked at the owner.

I stepped right in front of the Old Big and thanked him for the passage on his boat.

"You owe me money," he said, looking me straight in the eyes.

"But I paid the agreed sum in advance," I said. "I paid it all at Ichang."

"You owe me for food," he said in a surly way.

"It was agreed that food was included," I protested. "You agreed to that."

"Food is never included," the owner said.

I did not want to argue. At my age I wanted a sentimental parting. "How much?" I asked.

"Two taels."

"But that is impossible! That is half again the whole charge you made at Ichang."

"I lost my Noise Suppressor," the owner suddenly shouted, as if all his calamities were my fault. "I gave up a sampan. We have a bad mooring. The cook sleeps in my bed. What do you want, food for nothing?"

I paid the price and my guests sheepishly began to crowd out of the room. I could not engage Su-ling's eyes.

"Until again!" I said as cheerfully as I could.

"Until again," some of the boatmen mumbled, though they must have known, as I did, that there would never be an again.

I went to my room, and lay down, and for a short time suffered the blackest melancholy. I soon found myself reliving, all over again, those hours in Wind-Box Gorge; I lay wide awake, with my eyes tight closed, and once more every detail was vivid, stark, and personal. I do not know how long this went on. Suddenly, as I thought of the owner going after the drowning man in the light skiff on the awful water, I was gripped once again by the strange new sensation I had felt in the ferry-sampan crossing the river at dusk—a pang of wishing and despairing so strong that it both exalted and almost choked me. It was very strange. I began, with surprising speed, perhaps as a reaction to these violent feelings, to recover my spirits and, yes, my belief in the dam. This was just the first of it. Four months later I wrote an optimistic, even fervent, report on the possibilities of a dam in Yellow Cat Gorge, where, after further study, during a trip downriver by steamer, the site seemed to me best of all. It is clear that nothing ever came of that report, or of me. Indeed, my great career began and ended with that sheaf of papers. It was dismissed and I was tagged by sound men as impractical. The tag is still on me. The dam is still to be built. It will be, one day—of that I am sure. I feel now again, as I think back, the pang of wishing. I had it very strongly that night on the brick *k'ang* in the inn in Wanhsien, as I lay on my back on the hard bed turning over in my mind all that I had seen and felt on the river, and thinking of the head tracker and the owner and Su-ling and the cook and the others. I lay wide awake, aching and wishing. I could hear the buzz of the citizens of Wanhsien through the paper-paned window of my room. I heard an itinerant story-teller pass by with a crude shadow-scope, a kind of stereopticon that I had seen in towns downriver, and I heard him wail out his advertisements of famous things to be heard and seen at the modest charge of one round copper coin. Through distant streets wandered a timekeeper, beating on a gong the hours as they fled. All that night the Great River climbed the steps of the myriad city.

A Note on the TYPE

The text of this book was set on the Linotype in CALEDONIA, *a type face belonging to the family of printing types known to the printer as "modern face." This term, "modern," was used to mark the change in type-letter style that occurred at the end of the eighteenth century—a radical change in letter shapes evinced in the types designed by Bodoni, Baskerville, Martin, the Didots, and others.*

The book was composed by The Plimpton Press, Norwood, Massachusetts; printed and bound by H. Wolff, New York. The typography, decorations, and binding design were prepared by George Salter.